THOUGHTS OF *You*

THOUGHTS OF *You*

JANICE WILLIAMS

Primix Publishing
11620 Wilshire Blvd
Suite 900, West Wilshire Center, Los Angeles, CA, 90025
www.primixpublishing.com
Phone: 1-800-538-5788

Published by Primix Publishing   04/12/2022

ISBN: 978-1-957676-21-0(sc)
ISBN: 978-1-957676-22-7(e)

Contents

Dedication

To my son, David, who realized his dream of becoming an Air Force pilot. And to his late father, Robert, who will always be 'the wind beneath his wings.'

Prologue

Sometimes in life, we are fated to meet the one person who would change our lives forever. On a cold, foggy evening in London, Lieutenant Chase Morgan was destined to have such an encounter. Entering a small, quaint pub, The Boar's Head, he would surprisingly meet the girl of his dreams.

After graduating from the Air Force Academy in 1970, Chase received his first assignment, a Royal Air Force Base in England. Anxious to immerse himself in the local culture, he decided London would be the perfect place to start. Inviting his buddy, Lieutenant Christian Sanchez, they anxiously waited for their first weekend off duty. The young lieutenants took the train into the bustling metropolitan city and mapped out the numerous tourist attractions. Trafalgar Square seemed the perfect place to start. It offered spectacular views of Nelson's Column, the monument built to commemorate Admiral Horatio Nelson. Afterward, leisurely strolling along the winding cobblestone streets, they visited Piccadilly Circus, Tower Bridge, and the Tower of London as the evening sun slowly began to fade.

Suddenly, a thick fog rolled over the damp, narrow alleyway, consuming them in a fine mist. As darkness suddenly plummeted the temperature, Chase quickly buttoned his coat. Wrought-iron street lamps came on, illuminating their path. In the distance, a sign at the end of the street beckoned them. It announced their arrival at the Boar's Head Pub, established in 1810. From an outward appearance, it seemed somewhat disheveled. However, the glow radiating from the small mottled windows appeared inviting. Walking inside, the warmth of a coal fire felt invigorating. The pub's ambiance felt timeless as they took a seat in a booth near the back of the room. An appealing old-world charm and decayed stone interior gave the appearance that nothing had changed in the past hundred and sixty years. Looking at the drink menu, they decided to once again immerse themselves in the local culture by ordering tall mugs of New Castle Brown Ale. The aroma of meat pasties and bangers with mash permeated the air.

Surprisingly, Chase could never have known their decision to stop at the Boar's Head this evening would be life-changing.

Chapter One

On a damp, foggy night, in a small quaint bar tucked away in the heart of London, they met. Staring at her from across the room, Chase was mesmerized. Instantly, he had to know everything about her. Even from a distance, her petite, hourglass figure and golden blonde curls were captivating. Trying to exude an air of confidence, he walked over.

"My eyes were drawn to you the moment I saw you. Would you and your friend like to join us for a drink?" he asked candidly. As the words flew out of his mouth, he knew it was the worst pick-up line he had ever used.

With his sudden approach, he missed the intense scrutiny of her bodyguard, who remained steadfast at the entrance.

"Perhaps," she smiled, turning to face him.

Intrigued by his tenacity and naivety, she found him charming, especially his American accent. He was incredibly handsome, tall with an amazing physique, and sporting a crew cut of jet black hair, making her decision easy. Staring into his deep blue eyes, his perfectly sculpted profile could effortlessly rival Adonis.

"I'm Chase, and this is my buddy, Christian. May I order drinks for you and your friend?" he questioned politely, sensing undeniable chemistry.

"Thanks. We'll both have a shandy. I'm Cassandra, and this is my friend, Darcy." However, unlike Cassandra, Darcy's fiery red hair and gregarious personality were quite the opposite of her friend.

Sliding into the worn wooden booth, Cassie found him attractive. Rarely, when accompanied by security, was she ever approached by men in public. However, she loved the sincerity of his invitation. Glancing toward her bodyguard standing next to the entrance, she laughed. It was evident the young men had no idea of her prominence.

"How long have you been in England?" Darcy questioned, taking a sip of her drink. She thought it hilarious that they had no clue of Cassandra's royal status.

"Just two weeks," Christian interjected with a smile. "We're stationed at RAF Mildenhall."

Intrigued by the young Americans' boldness, Cassie felt it would be harmless to know more about them. "What do you do at RAF Mildenhall?"

"Oh, we're both pilots," Chase remarked with a flirtatious wink. His answer was usually a hit with all the girls, and he was using it to its full advantage.

"What do you and your friend fly, and you can call me Cassie?"

"Well, Cassie," Chase paused with a smile, captivated by her appearance. "Christian and I fly jets, F-4 Phantoms."

Cassie was stunning, and Chase loved her genuine curiosity. The fact that she had inquired about his job made him smile. However, it appeared she was more curious than impressed at hearing they were both pilots. Never before had Chase met anyone like her, yet their conversation was comfortable and effortless.

"Please, just call me Chris," Christian interjected, staring into Darcy's sparkling green eyes. Taking a sip of his New Castle Brown Ale, he wiped the foamy brew from his mouth. Chris was tall, with dark brown hair and a gorgeous olive complexion. He mirrored Chase's physique. "Do you girls live in the area?" Waiting pensively for Darcy's response, Chris found her fascinating.

"You have no idea, do you?" Darcy snickered, pointing in the direction of the bodyguard. "See the older gentleman standing near the front door."

"Oh, the strange guy in the suit who looks out of place?" Chris questioned.

"Yes. That's Roland, Cassie's bodyguard."

"Why does she need a bodyguard?"

Glancing at Cassie, the instant their eyes met, Chris felt foolish and naive. Apparently, there was a lot he didn't know about these beautiful young women, especially Cassie.

Lost in the depths of Cassie's azure blue eyes, Chase also felt there was something undeniably distinguished about her. However, he was taken entirely by surprise at Darcy's following comment.

"May I introduce my friend, Lady Cassandra Cromwell of Cambridge," Darcy stated.

"Oh my God," Chris stammered as ale spewed from his mouth. Shocked by the sudden announcement, he reached for a napkin, trying not to choke as he hid his embarrassment.

"Well, I must say the last thing I expected today was to meet someone of nobility," Chase grinned. "I have to ask what brought you into a local pub, especially on a night like this?"

Cassie frowned. "Are you saying we're not entitled to mix with the locals, and you have further complaints about our weather?"

"Oh, certainly not," Chase responded, worried his questions overstepped the confines of protocol.

The last thing he wanted was to offend the gorgeous girl sitting across from him. He felt like the luckiest guy on earth at this very moment.

"Darcy has an apartment in Chelsea, and I often visit," Cassie smiled. "However, you're right. It is unusual for us to be in a local pub at this time of night. Surprisingly as it might seem, as we drove past, it just compelled us to come inside for a shandy. We hadn't expected to encounter anyone personally. I meant it's unexpected that anyone would dare to approach our table with security nearby. However, I must say, I found your invitation bold and intriguing," Cassie explained, entirely fascinated by the young pilot.

Americans were known to be brash, and yet she found Chase charming. More often than not, just one glance towards her security, and she could have easily had the young men ushered to the door. Either way, he would have become a victim of her entourage. However, tonight that was not to be the case. They seemed fated to meet.

"Wow, I guess this changes things. A lot," Chris grimaced, feeling a bit intimidated.

"Really, is that how you feel?" Darcy questioned, taking a sip of her drink.

"Chris, speak for yourself," Chase smiled, totally enchanted.

"Trust me, if I wanted you to leave, you would already be tossed out on your ears," Cassie giggled. "Where are you from in the states?"

"I'm from Denver, Colorado, and Chris is from Miami, Florida."

"Those cities are not in the same state. How did the two of you meet?"

"Oh, at the Air Force Academy, we were fortunate enough to receive the same assignment, RAF Mildenhall," Chase answered. "We're roommates. We rent a small row house in Mildenhall. It's a better choice than living on base in the barracks with all the animals," he smirked.

"Cassie, we better be going," Darcy interrupted, looking down at her watch. "It's almost 8:30 p.m. It's late. Your parents always ring the flat before they retire for the evening." Hurriedly finishing the last of her shandy, Darcy appeared ready to bolt for the door.

"Darcy, calm down. The car is waiting outside. Your flat is only two blocks away on High Street. We'll make it before they ring." Cassie desperately wanted more time with the handsome American.

"Can I see you again?" Chase inquired.

With his impudence, Cassie knew he wasn't about to let her get away quickly and without a way to contact her.

"You can't directly ring Cassie, but I'll convey a message for you. Here's the number to my flat," Darcy interrupted, anxiously writing her phone number on a paper napkin.

"Yes, that would work," Cassie agreed. "You have no idea the control my family tries to impose on my life."

"Unfortunately, she's right," Darcy laughed, sliding the napkin across the table. "You have neither a title of nobility or the right DNA pulsing through your veins, which would allow you to date, Cassie. And you're an American. Her dad hates Yanks. Sorry, I didn't mean to be so blunt."

"Please, don't bother yourself with Darcy's rude comments. She's just overprotective," Cassie apologized. "I would love for you to ring me up."

Watching as the buff bodyguard walked over to usher the girls out of the pub, Chase inaudibly mouthed the words, "I'll call you."

"Wow, you're going to call her, aren't you?" Chris frowned, watching as the girls walked out of the pub. "Buddy, I'm sorry, but she's way out of your league. Are you crazy?"

"Just crazy enough," Chase countered with a grin, downing a huge gulp of the dark ale. "Our meeting tonight wasn't a coincidence, and there's no doubt I'm going to see her again."

Chapter Two

The following day, they were back in Mildenhall. The weekend was almost over. Lounging back on their shabby, worn sofa, Chase lit a cigarette. Thoughts of Cassie consumed him.

Bounding down the stairs, Chris was dressed in sweatpants and a baggy sweatshirt depicting the academy logo. He was on his way to the base gym, where he would spend a few hours working out. Reaching the bottom step, he stopped.

"Oh, my God, buddy, just an hour with that girl, and she's got you tied up in knots. I'm afraid you are in big trouble. Take a bit of friendly advice, and put her out of your mind," Chris vented, searching for his gym bag. "You're in over your head," he yelled from the kitchen. "Seriously, snap out of it. You don't stand a chance. The sooner you get that through your thick skull, the better. Damn! You're not listening to a word I've said. Go change."

"Chris, I don't need one of your brainless lectures. I'm going to call Darcy this evening. I've got to see Cassie. I just have to figure out the logistics," Chase snapped, extinguishing his cigarette.

"Whatever, buddy, but don't say I didn't warn you. We came here to fly jets, not get besotted by a couple of gorgeous Brits, as the blokes would say. I might remind you that one of them was English nobility,

Lady Cassandra Cromwell of Cambridge," Chris laughed hysterically. "Now, get over it. Let's go."

Driving back from the base, after an extensive workout, they were both starving. Chris was anxious to taste the famed local cuisine suggesting a stop at the local fish and chips. After all, you didn't come over without trying it, and they had already been in England for two weeks.

Walking into the small shop, the aroma of hot grease and fried battered fish wafted heavily in the air. It was intoxicating. After quickly surveying the menu, they ordered cod and chips with a side order of pickled onions. Receiving their battered fillets wrapped in newspapers, they were amused. "Wow, that's different," Chase laughed.

"Yes, but it looks amazing." Quickly unwrapping the greasy cover, Chris devoured a large piece of the crispy fish. "Oh, my gosh, this stuff is incredible."

"You're right. It's delicious," Chase agreed, tasting the popular delicacy as he reached for the malt vinegar, covering his fish with the condiment.

"Man, these are tasty, but you're killing it with the vinegar," Chris laughed, popping a pickled onion in his mouth.

"You enjoy it your way. I love the taste of malt vinegar. I don't think I've ever tasted anything so phenomenal."

"Okay, buddy, if it works for you," Chris laughed, watching as Chase continually drenched his fillet with the light brown liquid.

They were instant fans of the famed cuisine, consuming their last morsels of fish and chips.

"Geez, I never knew something so basic could taste this good," Chris mentioned.

"I foresee lots of fish and chips in our future," Chase grinned, wiping his mouth. "Especially since neither of us likes to cook."

"Finally, you're in a better mood," Chris remarked, hoping that Chase had given up any thoughts of contacting Cassie as they walked outside.

"Well, maybe, but I'm still calling Darcy later tonight."

"Okay, but don't say I didn't warn you when you 'crash and burn.'"

Arriving back at the apartment, Chris quickly ran upstairs to the shower.

"Don't forget, tomorrow we have to be at the base early for the training mission. Who's your weapons system officer for tomorrow's flight?"

"Oh, McDonald, Mad Dog," Chase yelled as Chris bounded up the stairs.

"Well, better you than me. My wizzo for tomorrow is D'Amario. I swear I love that guy. He's hilarious, and even though he's not a graduate of the academy, he's incredible. See you in the morning."

Reaching for the phone, Chase decided to call Darcy. Hopefully, with a bit of luck, she would be available.

After four rings, Darcy finally answered.

"Hello."

"Darcy, this is Chase. Do you have a few minutes?"

"Well, if it isn't the lieutenant," Darcy answered gingerly. "I figured you would call sooner or later. You're all that Cassie talks about."

"Really? To be honest, I can't get her out of my mind."

"Figures. She has a crush on you, but she'd kill me for telling you," Darcy snickered.

"I want to see her."

"You do know that's going to be impossible. If I can offer you some advice, I think you should forget about Cassie. Trust me. You have no idea how different her life is from yours."

"Listen, Darcy. I didn't call to get your advice. I just want to see her. Would you please let her know?"

"Geez, I must be as mad as a bag of ferrets for going along with this, but I'll see what I can do. I'm not making any promises. Why don't you give me a ring tomorrow evening? I'll get in touch with Cassie and let her know you called."

"Thanks, Darcy. You're awesome. I'll call you tomorrow."

Hanging up the phone, Chase smiled. Perhaps, there was a glimmer of hope.

Waking early the following day to the sound of his alarm clock, Chase ran for the shower. He wanted to get in and out of the bathroom before Chris. He was notorious for spending hours in the bathroom, and this morning they were up against a time crunch. Quickly taking a shower and getting dressed, Chase ran downstairs to make coffee. He knew the aroma of hot brewed coffee would wake Chris from his deep slumber.

"Hey, man, why didn't you wake me when you got up?" Chris questioned, rubbing his eyes as he strolled into the kitchen. Then, reaching for a large mug, he poured himself a cup of the hot brew.

"Because I didn't want to wait for you to get out of the bathroom. Honestly, you're like a girl. You take forever."

"Geez, Buddy, that's a low blow. How did your call with Darcy go? You did call her last night, right?"

"Of course."

"Damn, you're seeing her again."

"I certainly hope so, but Darcy is my go-between right now. I'm going to call her tonight and see if she can get in touch with Cassie."

"Well, good luck with that. I think you know my opinion on the subject of Cassie. As I said, you're out of your league. Way out of your league, I might add."

"Geez," Chase smirked. "You're just like Darcy. You're both madder than a bag of ferrets. I believe that was the phrase she used last night."

"A bag of ferrets," Chris laughed as coffee spewed from his mouth. "That's too funny. The guys will love that one. You're certainly picking up the British slang," he added, reaching for a napkin.

"Chris, there's no mention of Cassie around the guys. I'm serious."

"Okay, calm down, don't get your feathers ruffled so early in the morning," Chris countered. "Just know, your connection to this girl is going nowhere."

"Well, I'm not asking for your advice, so no more comments regarding Cassie. Get dressed. We have to be at the squadron in less than an hour. Sometimes, I feel like your mother instead of your roommate," Chase scowled.

Driving out to the RAF base, they soaked in the local scenery. The sun's early morning rays were just beginning to make their appearance as it vividly bathed the sky in hues of bright orange and pink. Glancing at the English countryside gave the impression of a large green quilt pieced together within stone borders that were now crumbling due to age. Dew glistened above the fields as it slowly dissipated from the sun's warmth.

"There's a lot to be said about the beauty of this country. However, I think the single-track roads are treacherous."

"Well, I suggest you keep your eyes on the road. They're narrow, and driving on the opposite side is unnerving. It was a smart move on your part to purchase Captain Warren's Mini Cooper when he rotated back to the states. The Brits are right. Yank tanks barely fit on these roads, especially the single-track roads. Damn, Chase, keep your eyes on the road. You almost sideswiped that lorry."

"Geez, Chris, get a grip. Seriously, you're about to take the controls of a jet, and you seem unusually nervous."

"Trust me. I can easily handle a jet at Mach 2. It's your driving that scares the hell out of me."

Saluted as they entered RAF Mildenhall, they were only a few blocks from their squadron, where they received daily briefings before their training missions.

Later, as they walked toward the flight line and a row of F-4 Phantoms, Chase looked forward to his time in the air. His love of flying was paramount to everything in his life except Cassie. As he climbed into the cockpit, the crew chief walked around the plane, making his final inspections. Finally, removing the chocks from under the tires, he motioned Chase toward the runway. Looking over at Chris, piloting the Phantom next to him, he put on his helmet. Quickly going over his checklist as the canopy closed, Chase gave the young airman a quick thumbs up. He was excited to get his plane in the air, even if Mad Dog McDonald was seated behind him as the wizzo for today's mission. His only concern was getting in crucial hours of training, which would desperately be needed if he received orders for a tour of duty in Southeast Asia.

After a routine training exercise, they arrived back at the squadron. Finally, with the debriefing over, the guys were ready to hit the Officer's Club and enjoy a pint of New Castle. It provided a place to unwind with the boys, have fun, and tease the pilots who made minor mistakes during the exercise.

After downing only one pint of New Castle, thoughts of Cassie made Chase anxious to leave. He had other things on his mind, which didn't include flying or anything related.

"Are you ready to go?" Chase questioned, walking over to Chris.

"Geez, we just got here. Why don't you go? I'll catch a ride with Lieutenant Stevenson."

"Suit yourself. I'm out of here," Chase grinned, a bit perturbed, walking toward the door.

"So, what's up with Chase?" Mad Dog questioned with a smirk.

"Oh, he's in love," Chris laughed after Chase left the building. "Just like a lovesick puppy."

"What? We've only been here for about two weeks. How's that even possible?"

"I guess some of us just get lucky. But trust me, Chase will never get to first base with this one," Chris added, downing a slow sip of ale. He was about to do the one thing Chase had explicitly asked him not to do, which was to mention Cassie.

"Really, what gives?" Mad Dog was determined to know everything, and he knew Chris had consumed just enough ale to tell him without thought of the consequences.

"Well, it's almost unbelievable," Chris continued. "Had I not been there, I probably wouldn't believe it myself. Chase and I went to London last weekend. You know, doing the tourist thing. We stopped at a local pub. Two girls walked in, and I swear before they could even order a drink, Chase walked over and invited them to join us."

"I certainly don't see anything wrong with that picture," Mad Dog grinned, ordering another Guinness.

"What I haven't told you is that one of the girls is English nobility. She even had a bodyguard waiting at the door. Unexpectedly, we had met Lady Cassandra Cromwell of Cambridge, and Chase thinks he's in love with her. No, I take that back," Chris hesitated, lifting the pint of ale to his mouth. "He's in love with her."

"Oh, my God," Mad Dog laughed hysterically. "Damn, that's the funniest thing I've ever heard. Hey, Stevenson, did you hear that? Chase is in love with a princess," Mad Dog roared.

"I didn't say a princess," Chris corrected. "I said her title was Lady Cassandra Cromwell."

"Ahh, that's frigging hilarious," Lieutenant Zac Stevenson laughed, almost choking on his beer.

Thanks to Chris, practically everyone in Chase's squadron knew or would know that he was in love with Cassie once the word got around. Without Chase's knowledge, he had just become the focus of entertainment. Now, Chris would have to suffer the repercussions of his actions.

"Hey Chris, I'm leaving. Didn't you say you needed a ride?" Zac inquired.

"Yes."

Driving into Mildenhall, Zac worried about Chris.

"Chris, isn't Chase your roommate? I don't mean to pry, and I'm not trying to get into your business, but I think Mad Dog was the last person you should have confided in. You know his reputation. I'm afraid you might not have a roommate if Chase finds out."

"You might be right. I can't believe I told Mad Dog. Damn. Maybe, if I'm lucky, Chase won't find out."

"Are you joking? I wouldn't hold out much hope on that. However, if you need a place to stay, you're welcome to come over and crash on the couch. I'm sure Karen wouldn't mind," Zac offered as he stopped in front of the quaint row house.

"Thanks for the offer to crash on your sofa and the ride home. See you tomorrow."

Walking in, Chase was on the phone. Trying to sneak past him without being noticed, Chris discretely headed upstairs. Chase was the last person he wanted to encounter.

Waking the following day to the robust coffee aroma, Chris put on his bathrobe and walked downstairs to the kitchen. Neither of them had to report to the base until later that afternoon.

"Did you hear from Cassie?" Chris asked, curiously pouring himself a cup of coffee.

"Yes, as a matter of fact, I did. I called Darcy."

"So, what's up?" Chris asked, taking a sip of the hot brew.

"You're not going to believe this, but George, the family chauffeur, is driving Cassie up to Mildenhall. Cambridge is only twenty-four miles away, and we figured there was less chance of her being recognized here."

"Wow, that's great. How did Cassie manage to get the approval of her parents?"

"Well, that's a different story. I never said Cassie had their approval."

"Chase, do you know what you're doing? Damn, Buddy, you could be jeopardizing your military career as a pilot if you get involved with someone of her status. Especially if her parents happen to find out and disapprove."

"Chris, she's twenty-two years old. She doesn't have to have their approval. The fact that she's from a family of prominence might be a significant concern, but I'm going to see her. I'm seeing her," Chase repeated. "Damn it, Chris, that's the end of it. I don't need your approval to live my life."

"Chase, I'm sorry. I'm only scared that you're in over your head. I worry about you."

"Chris, no one asked you to worry about me," Chase snapped, furiously pouring himself another cup of coffee.

"Okay, I'll say no more about Cassie. You have my word."

Taking a deep breath, Chris couldn't believe the words that had flown out of his mouth the previous evening at the Officer's Club. He hadn't kept his promise. He knew their friendship could be over if Chase found out, and he wasn't ready to deal with it. However, Chris had dodged a bullet, at least for now, as Mad Dog received a temporary duty assignment to Spain for the remainder of the week.

"I think I might go for a short run. Want to join me?" Chris had to get out of the house.

"No. Enjoy your run. I've got some letters to write back home. They're long overdue."

Grabbing pen and paper, Chase walked into the living room and lounged back on the sofa as Chris headed upstairs to change.

Gathering his thoughts, Chase had a lot to write home about.

His fabulous weekend in London would make a great place to start. However, there would be no mention of Cassie. For the time being, his friendship with her was best kept merely between the four of them, Cassie, Darcy, Chris, and himself.

If things progressed the way Chase hoped, he might have more news to share with his mom. The weekend was fast approaching, and he couldn't wait to see Cassie.

Chapter Three

Saturday finally arrived, and not a moment too soon. Chase was ecstatic. Nervously pacing the floor, he downed several cups of coffee. Looking at the clock, it was almost 5:00 p.m. Finally, hearing a soft knock at the door, he took a deep breath and walked over. Opening the door, Cassie appeared radiant. Wearing her beautiful blond curls swept back, it revealed exquisite diamond earrings. She was stunning.

"Wow, you're here," Chase paused, overwhelmed at the mere sight of her.

"Well, are you going to invite me in?"

"Yes, of course. What about your driver, George? Is he waiting?"

"Oh, I told him to drop me off. He'll return in a few minutes."

"Hurry, come inside. Would you like something to drink?"

"No, silly. Sit down. You look nervous," Cassie laughed. "Where's your roommate, Chris?"

"Oh, Chris, he's at the gym." Chase was so nervous. He almost forgot the fact that he had a roommate.

"I can't stay long, but I have a plan. Darcy's parents have a beach house in Hunstanton. It's only about forty miles. What do you think about spending the weekend on the beach? The house is remote, and

Darcy gave me a key. No one is there, and we'll have the entire place to ourselves."

"Are you kidding? It sounds fantastic." Chase couldn't fathom his luck. "Is George staying for the weekend?"

"Yes, but he's just dropping us off. His sister lives nearby, in Isleham, and he's staying with her. I asked George to pick us up in ten minutes. I was hoping you might say yes."

Peeping through the curtains, Cassie smiled, noting George's return.

"A beach house," Chase questioned, not believing his luck as he ran upstairs, grabbing a change of clothes. The afternoon had unexpectedly turned into a weekend.

"George is here," Cassie announced.

"Cassie, that's a taxi," Chase remarked, looking out the window.

"I know. Isn't it cool? What would you prefer? A limo. I think that would be too conspicuous," she laughed. "The taxi was George's idea. He borrowed it from a friend, and he's going to drive us out to Hunstanton Beach. You're going to love him. If it weren't for George and his ability to provide convincing alibis for me, I would have no social life."

"Wow, he sounds like a great guy." Taking Cassie's hand, they ran down the narrow steps leading to the car.

George held the door for them as they discreetly got into the back seat.

"I have to know. What did you tell your parents?"

"Oh, they know that I'm going to the beach house for the weekend. However, they think Darcy is there. They have no idea that George borrowed a taxi or that I came by to pick you up. Kinda perfect, isn't it?"

"Brilliant, but where's your bodyguard?"

"Oh, Roland? We left him at his flat in Cambridge. Don't worry about him. He's a neat guy. Roland has been covering for Darcy and me since we turned eighteen. A girl has to have some privacy," Cassie smirked.

"Wasn't he with you at the pub?"

"Yes, but my parents were also in London. I was just staying overnight with Darcy."

"Geez, your life sounds complicated."

"Oh, you have no idea," Cassie smiled, snuggling closer.

Pulling her into his arms, Chase couldn't resist giving her a quick kiss on her forehead. He couldn't believe they were together and would have the entire weekend alone.

It was only a short thirty-minute drive out to the coast. Arriving at the beach house, it was a sprawling two-story structure.

"Wow, does everyone live this lavish?"

"Umm, I'm not sure. However, everyone I know does," Cassie laughed.

The house's exterior beautifully revealed weathered shingles with decks that wrapped the entire structure. Turquoise blue awnings covered each window, and a gorgeous stained glass door complemented its outward appearance.

"Cassie, there are lights on in the house. I thought you said no one was here?"

"Well, that's strange," Cassis commented, looking closer. "Darcy assured me we had the place to ourselves. She must have had someone stop by and ensure the house was ready for our arrival."

Driving up to the entrance, George parked. Opening their door, he waited for them to exit the taxi. Retrieving Cassie's luggage, he sat her bags next to the front door.

"If you need me, call this number."

"Thanks, George. Tell your sister I said hello," Cassie added.

"I will. Please try to stay out of trouble. I wouldn't relish the idea of trying to explain this to your parents."

"Thank you, George. It was nice to meet you," Chase added, picking up Cassie's bags.

"Enjoy your stay. I'll return on Sunday afternoon."

Unlocking the door, Cassie gasped. The entire bottom floor glowed from the illumination of lit lanterns and the aroma of candles. A magnum of champagne sat near the fireplace, a bucket of ice, and two fluted glasses.

"Wow, Darcy, I swear she knows how to fix a girl up. It's so romantic."

"It looks amazing," Chase commented, setting their luggage inside the foyer.

Taking off her shoes, Cassie ran into the kitchen. A gorgeous granite island sat in the middle of the large room. Dark mahogany cabinetry surrounded an expensive AGA cooker accessorized with an ornate copper range hood. The kitchen and family room had enclosed glass panels that opened to allow the fresh ocean breeze to waft inside and showcased a complete panorama.

"Geez, this kitchen is enormous," Chase laughed.

Opening the fridge, Cassie gasped.

"Yum! Chocolate-covered strawberries, Darcy didn't miss a thing. I love chocolate. There's enough food in here to last for weeks," she added, surveying the fridge's contents. "Let's take these into the living room," she suggested removing the tray of strawberries.

Following Cassie into the living room, Chase removed his shoes as he walked over to inspect the fireplace. An ample supply of logs was stored nearby. It would be the perfect way to warm up the spacious room.

"Why don't I start a fire? There's plenty of wood, and it's quite cool and overcast outside."

"Great idea. I'm going to change into something more comfortable," Cassie stated, setting the tray of strawberries on an oversized ornate coffee table. Reaching for her bags, Chase immediately stopped her.

"Wait, I'll take those upstairs for you."

"Thanks. You can set them inside the primary bedroom. I'll be down in a few minutes.

"Okay," Chase replied, following behind her with the luggage.

Heading downstairs, Chase stopped midway on the steps to view the massive living room. Scratching his head, he couldn't fathom people living this extravagant on the beach. Tall vaulted ceilings with exposed wooden beams traversed the entire length of the living area. The massive stone fireplace centered the room, and expansive windows towered upward, revealing gray swirling clouds moving inward from the ocean. Despite its size, the room's ambiance made it feel cozy and comfortable.

After starting a roaring fire, Chase opened the champagne and filled two fluted glasses. If the guys at work could only see him now, he thought.

Watching as Cassie slowly descended the stairs, she took his breath away in her bare feet, wearing a black halter mini dress. She was a vision of beauty.

"Wow, you look exquisite," he winked, meeting her at the bottom step.

"Thanks. You look pretty handsome yourself."

"Oh, I'm not so sure about that, but I managed to get the fire going," Chase laughed, handing her a glass of champagne. "Why don't we enjoy those yummy chocolate-covered strawberries you love."

Taking the comfy throw pillows from the sofa, Chase tossed them on the floor in front of the warm, crackling fire. Gently slipping his arm around Cassie's petite waist, the floral scent of her perfume was hypnotic. Pulling her down next to him, Cassie snuggled into his strong muscular arms.

"Tell me everything there is to know about you, Casandra Cromwell," Chase questioned, taking a sip of champagne. "Everything," he added.

"Oh, I'm not sure you would find my life interesting."

"Sweetheart, from the looks of this place, I'd say there's a lot to know."

"Chase, one thing you need to understand is money, and material things have never impressed me. Trust me, I've had just about everything money can buy, and I've traveled the world more than once, and not one of those things without someone to share them with has ever brought me happiness. Not one."

"Geez, Cassie, that's quite a statement. That's the saddest thing I've ever heard. I'm afraid you'll find my life boring."

"Chase, your past isn't important to me. But, your audacity drew me to you that night," she laughed. "The fact you were bold enough to walk over and invite me to join you." Taking a sip of champagne, Cassie nuzzled closer. "Your actions revealed a lot about your character."

"Well, considering I didn't know who you were at that time, it might make that statement insignificant," Chase laughed, pulling her closer into his arms.

"Chase, I'm sure you're going to think this sounds entirely absurd, but I've been unhappy most of my life. You can have a title in front of your name and all that goes with it and feel completely miserable and alone."

"Cassie, again, that's the saddest thing ever, especially coming from someone of your prominence," he paused, entirely caught off guard by her comment.

"Told you," she answered, burying her head against his chest to cover a tear that unexpectedly escaped her moist eyes.

Caressing her face with his hands, Chase lovingly kissed away the tears trickling down her cheeks.

"Sweetheart, what if I told you that I think we were fated to meet. I felt it with every ounce of my being when I saw you that night. Do you believe in love at first sight?"

"I suppose. It's possible. I've never met anyone like you," Cassie replied demurely, wiping her eyes. "It's strange, but I felt very comfortable when I met you, and I was hoping you would contact Darcy. I wanted to see you again."

"Well, that's a start, and I can live with that for now," Chase laughed. "At least, it's something to build our relationship around, and the fact you didn't hate me for being so bold to approach you without knowing your title."

"Chase, oddly enough, I found it quite refreshing that you had no idea of my identity, and hate is a strong word. I could never hate you," Cassie smiled. "It's quite the opposite."

"Now, that's my girl. I love it when you smile. You haven't touched the strawberries. Why don't I prepare dinner? I love to cook, and you like to eat, right?" he teased, kissing her forehead.

"Chase, you're silly, but I love you."

Cassie had surprisingly used the word *love*. Trying to grasp what happened, she froze, unable to speak. The word had slipped innocently from her heart.

"Oh, I'm sorry. It must be the champagne," she blushed.

"Sweetheart, now you're the one being silly. Sometimes, the truest words are spoken from the heart," Chase smiled, gently pulling a loose strand of hair away from her face.

Cassie had no idea the effect she was having on him.

Taking her glass, Chase sat it on the coffee table. Pulling Cassie closer, he kissed her with sudden, intense passion.

Never having experienced this feeling with anyone, Cassie felt safe. Melting into Chase's embrace, she felt as if she could stay in his arms forever.

"Wow, I think I better cook dinner," Chase whispered, staring into her gorgeous blue eyes.

"I suppose you should know that I hate cooking?" Cassie laughed. "Remember, you said you wanted to know everything."

"Cassie, there are so many things I love about you. Trust me, cooking doesn't even make the top ten," Chase winked, pulling her to his chest for another quick kiss. "Geez, sweetheart, if we continue, we might starve."

"Food is overrated," Cassie whispered, returning his kisses with sizzling enthusiasm. Being held in Chase's arms, she felt breathless. There was no doubt she was falling in love with the young lieutenant.

Taking advantage of the moment, dinner soon became insignificant, merely a quick second thought. Chase removed the diamond clasp allowing her long blonde tresses to fall softly around her shoulders. Gently loosening her halter, he kissed the nape of her neck. "You're gorgeous," Chase whispered. Even though he was madly in love with Cassie, he hesitated for a brief moment before taking things further. The mere fact that she was British nobility meant he wasn't moving their relationship to a physical one without knowing she felt the same.

"Hush, make love to me before I change my mind."

As the morning light filtered into the massive room, Cassie slowly opened her eyes. Tiny burning embers in the fireplace were all that remained of the roaring fire from the previous night, leaving a coolness in the air. Staring at the handsome guy who still slept peacefully beside her, she snuggled closer. The warmth of his body and the fact that she had someone in her life were euphoric. Kissing Chase awake, he pulled her into his arms.

"Wow, Sweetheart, what a night," he winked, wickedly giving her a quick kiss.

"Yes, lieutenant, you're right. It was amazing," Cassie smiled, lovingly caressing Chase's face, now covered in a hint of dark stubble. "Thanks for the warm blanket."

"I was going to carry you upstairs, but you were sleeping peacefully, and I didn't want to wake you, so I removed one of the comforters to keep you warm."

"I'm starved. I remember you saying last night you liked to cook. Does that include making breakfast?"

"Of course, why don't I make coffee, and you decide what sounds good."

"Oh, poached eggs, bacon, and toast."

"That was an easy decision. Why don't you shower and dress? I'll get things started in the kitchen," Chase smiled, grabbing his clothes.

Pulling the comforter around her petite frame, Cassie walked toward the stairs. Trying not to trip, she had difficulty maneuvering the staircase with the heavy blanket in tow.

"Careful, Sweetheart, don't fall," he laughed, watching as she suddenly became entangled inside the comforter.

Instantly dropping the massive blanket, Cassie bolted up the remaining stairs, totally nude.

Unable to take his eyes off her, Chase loved Cassie's spontaneity. She never ceased to amaze him with her childish antics. He was more than ever falling in love with her.

"Wow, Lady Cassandra Cromwell, that's cute," Chase teased. "I better make coffee before I decide to follow you upstairs."

Brewing a pot of coffee became his priority. Next, he searched the cabinets for pots and pans and the fridge's contents. Finding all the ingredients he needed, it wasn't long before the aroma of fried bacon infused the air. Finally, Chase had things under control by placing slices of bread under the broiler and poaching two eggs.

Stepping out of the warm shower and pulling her hair into a ponytail, the smell of freshly brewed coffee and fried bacon instantly awakened Cassie's appetite. Reminded that they only had the chocolate-covered strawberries and champagne the previous evening, she felt ravenous. Deciding to grab a cozy bathrobe and slippers, Cassie was too hungry to worry about dressing for the day.

Walking into the kitchen, one look at Chase and her heart melted. Not only had he cooked breakfast, but the mere sight of him standing in front of the stove wearing tight denim jeans and a T-shirt, which revealed his rippled abs, made her feel like the luckiest girl on earth.

"I hope you're hungry," he smiled, instantly walking over to greet her with a quick kiss. A hint of vanilla and coconut fragrance infused her hair. "Geez, you smell amazing."

"Awww, thanks. Breakfast looks scrumptious."

"Well, I hope you'll still feel that way after tasting everything. How do you like your coffee? Sugar or cream?" Chase questioned, reaching for the coffee cups.

"Just cream."

Deciding to eat at the island, Chase pulled out the leather stool for Cassie as he sat the steaming hot brew in front of her. Returning to the stove, he heaped large portions of everything onto plates and sat next to her.

"Wow, this is wonderful," Cassie smiled, devouring slices of bacon. "Who taught you how to cook?"

"Well, I guess you could say it was my grandmother. She lived with us for many years until she passed. Mom and dad both worked, and, unfortunately, they were never home."

"Oh, I'm sorry. I suppose I was spoiled, having cooks and nannies. We had a full staff."

"No need to feel sorry. I told you that my life in no way compares to yours. However, I wouldn't change a thing," Chase reminded her, walking over to refill his coffee.

Cassie paused, finishing her last morsel of bacon. "It appears the weather has cleared this morning. What do you think about a long stroll along the beach after we clear away the dishes?"

"Sounds like fun? How often do you come to Hunstanton Beach?"

"Not often. My parents have several residences, one of which is a summer house on the Isle of Wight and a villa in Monte Carlo."

After cleaning the kitchen, Cassie ran upstairs to dress. Chase rummaged through his duffel, pulling out a denim jacket. The weather, even in August, was known to be quite chilly and unpredictable. Finally,

Cassie bounded down the stairs. Dressed in jeans and a matching blue denim jacket, she looked incredible.

"Sorry. I had to dry my hair. Wow, look at us. We match."

"Geez, you're right," Chase laughed, taking her hand as they headed in the direction of the walkway leading down to the beach.

The wind began to pick up as they approached the ocean even though the sun was shining. The fresh salt air felt invigorating despite the chill which wafted in from the water. Pulling Cassie closer to keep her warm, he locked his arms around her as they leisurely strolled along the sandy shore. Chase had only one thing on his mind. Despite the breathtaking views of the ocean and the waves gently washing ashore, it was the gorgeous young girl he held in his arms. After last night, Chase desperately had to know more about her. Being alone and without interruptions, it seemed like the perfect time. Chase knew he was falling in love with her. Despite Chris's warnings, he was determined to make their relationship work.

After leisurely strolling down the beach, Chase wanted answers. "Cassie, Darcy mentioned that your dad doesn't like Americans. I believe she used the word hate. Why would she have made that statement? I'm just curious."

Cassie stopped to gather her thoughts, dodging the continued onslaught of whitecaps as they washed ashore, leaving a foamy deposit.

"Wow, that's a rather complicated story," she paused, staring at Chase with a somewhat confused expression. "You want the long or short version?"

"Cassie, I only ask because I'm totally in love with you, and the fact I'm not someone your parents might want you with is cause for concern. But, just so you know, regardless of their opinions, it doesn't change my feelings toward you. Nothing has ever felt this right in my entire life. Sweetheart, you are my forever."

"Chase, I regret Darcy blurted that out. It was disrespectful. I truly mean that, but I'm afraid she was speaking the truth. I'm sorry. You have to know those are not my thoughts. They have never been and never will be. My dad, Ian, is just an angry, resentful man. Unrealistically, my entire family hated my Aunt Olivia, his younger sister, because she married an American. My Aunt Olivia married Uncle Kelsey against the wishes of my grandparents. She even moved to the states with him to escape their vile undertakings. Unfortunately, I was young at the time, and without knowing all the details, it might seem unfair to blame my uncle. From everything I know, I don't blame him. Aunt Olivia was my dad's only sister. She wanted out of the confinement of our lifestyle, and she chose him to accomplish it. She gave up her title, and the entire family disowned her. I'm afraid if Dad discovered the fact you're an American, he might easily do the same," Cassie explained as her eyes moistened.

"Cassie, I'm truly sorry," Chase sympathized. Taking the back of his hand, he wiped her moist face. "I didn't mean to upset you. Trust me, that was the last thing I wanted. I just needed to know."

"I understand, but you have to know that I'm not like my Aunt Olivia. She was the baby of the family, spoiled and privileged. Uncle Kelsey played polo for one of the local teams, and she met him after an event. He was ruggedly handsome and wealthy. He had all the attributes that Aunt Olivia was looking for, making her decision to marry him easy and relocate to the states. My dad hated her for leaving and blamed Uncle Kelsey for her poor choices."

"Sweetheart, thanks for sharing that part of your life with me. We're not your Aunt Olivia or Uncle Kelsey. Unfortunately, I'm not wealthy. I simply got my dream job flying for Uncle Sam. What were your dreams growing up? I mean outside of your family's title?"

Cassie's answers would have to wait until later. The wind rapidly became blustery as gray clouds appeared out of nowhere, swirling angrily overhead. A downpour of rain seemed imminent. It was time to turn back.

"Geez, where did that come from?" Chase laughed, grabbing Cassie's hand as they bolted in the direction of the beach house.

"The weather on the coast can change rapidly," Cassie giggled, holding tight to Chase's hand as they sprinted to safety.

Suddenly, the dark clouds released a heavy deluge of rain, soaking them to their core. Thoroughly drenched as they arrived back at the beach house, they quickly removed their wet shoes at the door and raced upstairs. A warm shower seemed their only option. Discarding their soaked clothes on the bathroom floor, Chase pulled Cassie inside the shower.

"Conserving water," Chase whispered, pulling Cassie into his arms as the warm water washed over them.

Cassie smiled, running her fingers through his hair, "shampoo?"

"Later," Chase winked, kissing her passionately.

The shower quickly became a private party for two. Thankfully, their weekend had surprisingly given them another chance to explore their feelings of love and intimacy due to the unexpected downpour. At this point, Chase was confident Cassie shared those feelings. However, after hearing Cassie's earlier explanation regarding her dad's true feelings, Chase could only hope to change her dad's sentiments.

Stepping outside the shower, they hurriedly dressed and raced downstairs, hoping to get a roaring fire started to stave off the coldness of the house.

"You start the fire, and I'll grab some glasses and the champagne," Cassie suggested standing on her toes to give him a quick kiss on his forehead.

Cassie returned a few minutes later with the champagne and an assortment of cheese, fruit, and crackers that would carry them until dinner. Feeling the warmth of the roaring fire, it immediately removed the chill from the room. Reaching for Cassie, Chase pulled her over as she set the tray on the coffee table. Pouring glasses of the sparkling beverage, they snuggled closer to the warmth of the roaring fire. Chase was anxious to continue their earlier conversation.

"I believe you were going to tell me all about your dreams and aspirations just before the rain caught us," Chase smiled with a flirtatious wink. "I told you my dream was to become a pilot. What was yours?"

"Well, if you must know, I always wanted to become a journalist for a large newspaper or magazine. I love writing."

"Wow, that's awesome. What stopped you?"

"Nothing has stopped me. It's more like I've put it on hold until the right time," Cassie paused, reflecting on her answer. Taking a sip of champagne, she grabbed a piece of cheese.

"I'm sure you would be great. I don't understand why you haven't pursued it further."

"Chase, there's still a lot you don't know. My mother, Jaclyn, has been quite ill over the past several years, and I'm the only child, so I've felt obligated to help with her care. We've always been close."

"I'm sorry. Is it serious? I don't mean to pry, and I'll understand if you'd rather not talk about it."

"It's okay. Yes, it's serious. Mom has advanced kidney disease, which requires dialysis. She's become quite frail, and I'm afraid of losing her."

"Sweetheart, I'm sorry. I had no idea."

"How could you have known? We've only been together for a short time," Cassie sighed.

Chase regretted that their conversation had resulted in such deep emotions. However, a change of subject was needed, and he felt responsible.

"Do you like spaghetti? I make a mean sauce. Why don't we check the cabinets? Hopefully, everything we need is in the kitchen?"

"Sounds good," Cassie eagerly agreed.

Quickly finding the needed ingredients, it wasn't long before the kitchen held the savory aroma of a superb Italian Bistro. The sauce was to perfection. Opening a Merlot bottle was the ultimate compliment to a meal that Chase hoped would leave a lasting impression. Opening another bottle, he grabbed two glasses as they retired back to the warmth of the fireplace.

After too many refills, Cassie fell asleep. Chase decided to gently carry her upstairs to the primary suite, trying not to wake her. Pulling back the heavy toile duvet, he slipped her beneath the covers. Deciding to sleep next to her, Chase cherished their remaining time together. Soon the sun would appear and signal the end of their fantastic weekend.

The following morning as they packed and readied for George's arrival, Chase knew one thing. It was the fact that he had to see her again. Not sure of the circumstances that would allow such lunacy regarding Cassie's father, he just knew he would go to any lengths to make it happen.

"Hope your stay was pleasant?" George questioned, stowing their luggage in the trunk.

"Unbelievable," Cassie smiled.

"Incredible," Chase agreed with a wink.

Cassie snuggled into his arms for the short ride back to Mildenhall. Finally, stopping in front of the row house, their weekend was over, but not before Cassie entertained the logistics of seeing Chase again.

"What are your plans for next weekend?"

"None that I'm aware of," Chase smiled inquisitively.

"Well, my parents are hosting a party on Saturday. Why don't you come as my guest?"

"I'm afraid I would be eaten alive?" Chase smirked.

"I would never let that happen. Trust me."

"It's not you that I'm worried about. It's your father."

"I think you'll survive. See you on Saturday. Oh, I'll call you with the details," Cassie smiled, giving Chase a quick passionate kiss.

"Saturday," Chase replied with a wink watching as George drove away.

Chapter Four

The interrogation began the moment Chase walked in.

"So, Romeo, how was your weekend?" Chris questioned.

"Unbelievable. I believe that's the word that comes to mind," Chase remarked, sitting his duffle by the front door.

"Okay, let's have it. What happened?"

"Really, Chris, you act like my mother."

"Well, someone has to watch over you."

"You need to get a life and stop meddling with mine. We had a fantastic time. Does that answer your question? I need a drink?"

"I have a better idea. Why don't we drive into the base and play Racketball?"

"Okay, but not another word about my weekend. Got it?"

"Got it."

Arriving at the gym, Chris hoped none of the guys would be there after his last conversation at the Officer's Club. The last thing he wanted was trouble between him and Chase. He knew that Zac would remain loyal to his word. With Mad Dog now on a Temporary Duty Assignment, it only left a few others who might have overheard his conversation regarding Chase's relationship with Cassie. Grabbing their rackets from the car, Chris knew he would have to take his chances.

Holding his breath, they walked in. Quickly finding a locker to store their personal belongings, they appeared the only ones.

Warming up, it seemed Chase was on his game despite the long weekend. Quickly gaining fifteen points, he easily won the first match and the next. Things were not going well for Chris. Effortlessly, Chase won.

"Okay, the winner has to buy a round of drinks," Chris scoffed, walking off the court.

Showered and dressed, they were about to leave the gym when Chris's luck ran out. Lieutenant Riley walked in.

"Oh my God, if it isn't Lieutenant Morgan or lover boy," he laughed hysterically. "Mad Dog said you were in love with a princess. What the hell is that about?"

Mad Dog, true to his nature, had told everyone. Instantly, Chase lost control. Taking one look at Chris, he lunged toward him, hitting him with brute force square in the face. Blood spewed from his nose. "Find your way home. Damn, some friend you are," Chase yelled.

Reeling from the shock of Chase's aggression, Chris pinched his nose and ran for the men's room. Grabbing paper towels, he managed to stop the bleeding. However, one look in the mirror left no doubt he would have a black eye.

"Damn, I'm sorry," Lieutenant Riley frowned, walking in. "I feel responsible. Is there anything I can do?"

"Yes. Can you give me a ride?"

"Not a problem. Do you want to stop at the ER?"

"No. I should never have opened my mouth in front of Mad Dog. I was warned he couldn't be trusted. I guess I had this one coming."

"Well, I'm not sure about that, but yeah, Mad Dog has no discretion or filter, and he's the last person you should ever expect to keep anything confidential. Sorry. Guess you learned the hard way."

"Yeah. Lesson learned. Let's just hope Chase can find a little forgiveness in his heart, or I may be looking for a new place to live."

"You can always crash on our couch. I'm sure Megan wouldn't mind."

"Thanks for the offer, but I'll take my chances with Chase tonight."

It was only a short ride from the base to Mildenhall. Chris had no idea what awaited him. Hopefully, Chase wouldn't throw his stuff into the street before he had a chance to apologize. There was no sign of duffel bags on the sidewalk as they arrived at the row house. Perhaps, it was a good sign.

"Thanks for the ride. See you next week," Chris smiled as he gently rubbed his bruised cheek.

"You sure you're okay?"

"Yes. I'm fine. Thanks."

The door was unlocked as Chris entered the house. There was no way to know if Chase was home as they always parked in the alley behind the house. Chris would simply have to find the courage to face him. Now more than ever, he regretted discussing Chase's love life. An apology was in order.

"See you found a ride," Chase scoffed, downing a beer as he sat glued to the television.

"Damn, I'm sorry. I genuinely mean it. I know I promised not to say anything. Can you forgive me, and let's try to get past this?"

Waiting pensively for Chase's reply, Chris had no idea what his response might be. Chris could only hope it didn't end their friendship. They had made it through the academy together, earned their wings, and received the same assignment. The loss would be devastating for both of them, not to mention its effect on their work relationship. Keeping focused on the mission each day was paramount. There was no room for error or misjudgments flying F-4 Phantoms at Mach 2.

"Hell, I'm sorry. I didn't mean to lose my temper," Chase apologized. "You want a New Castle. I stopped by the Class Six and stocked up."

"Yeah, I suppose," Chris replied, taking a deep breath as he continued to the kitchen.

"Better put some ice on it while you're in there. From the looks of it, you're going to have quite a shiner."

Chris returned to the living room, grabbing a beer from the fridge and a bag of frozen peas for his eye. Lounging back on their worn second-hand sofa, he was relieved Chase could move past the incident.

"By the way, your mom called while you were at the beach house,"

Chris mentioned, holding the frozen peas over his eye with one hand and a beer in the other.

"Oh, really, what did she want?"

"Just checking on you, that's all?"

"What did you tell her?"

"Oh, nothing. That you were fine."

"Did you mention Cassie or the fact we were together for the weekend?"

"Chase, give me a little credit. I would never do that. Trust me."

"Well, after today, I'm not sure that I can. But," Chase paused, "if you did, I promise I'll find out."

"No worries. I said you were assigned alert duty this weekend."

"Thanks. I'm going upstairs to call Darcy to see if she can reach Cassie. After that, I'm turning in for the night. See you in the morning. By the way, you might want to pick up some concealer tomorrow. Your eye looks terrible."

"Yeah. Well, thanks to you, I'll probably need it."

"Sorry."

The following week at work, it appeared that both Chase and Chris were the topics of discussion. However, no one dared to mention Cassie. The weekend was fast approaching, and Chase couldn't wait to see her, even though the worries of meeting her father were never far from his mind. It appeared the party wasn't formal, so there would be no need for proper attire. However, hoping to make a good impression, Chase chose to wear a suit minus the tie. Anxious to see Cassie, it felt like an eternity since their last weekend together.

As Chase entered the long circular drive, which led to the sprawling manor house entrance, the stately home's enormity was impressive, even under cover of darkness. Ivy covered the stone exterior, excluding the tall Tudor windows, which lined both the bottom and upper levels. Handing his keys to the attendant, Chase nervously approached the door. Fortunately, Cassie had noticed his arrival from her room upstairs and ran down to greet him.

"Hey, I'm glad you made it," Cassie giggled, quickly leading him through the house without being noticed and outside to the back terrace.

Decorative wrought iron lamps gave a warm glow to the ample outdoor space. The calming sound of water trickled from a large ornate fountain.

"Wow, your home is beautiful, and you look gorgeous."

"Thanks. Shush, no one knows you're here," Cassie whispered. "I just had to get you alone before the madness begins. You look incredible. You have no idea how much I've missed you," Cassie smiled, pulling him close.

"Stop talking and kiss me," Chase winked with a smile, wrapping her in his arms.

As their lips met, the passion emanating from Chase's kiss sent shivers throughout Cassie's petite body, leaving her weak in the knees. The fragrance of his cologne was hypnotic, hinting at spice and sandalwood.

"I've missed you too," Chase whispered. "Do we have to go inside? Can't we stay out here? Just the two of us."

"No. I'm sorry. Let's go inside, and I'll introduce you to my parents. After dinner, we can sneak back to the terrace."

Cassie grabbed his hand and led him toward the tall glass doors leading into the house.

"Don't be nervous."

"Geez, do I bow when I meet them?"

"Don't be silly. It's just a casual dinner party with a few close family friends. Just follow my lead. You'll be fine."

Chase was tense, knowing her father's disdain for Americans. He followed Cassie into the living room and toward a massive baroque fireplace.

"Chase, this is my father, the Earl of Cromwell, and my mother, the Countess of Cromwell."

"I'm pleased to meet you," Chase smiled with a slight nod.

Before uttering a word, Earl Cromwell stared at Chase for what seemed like an eternity. Still, in reality, it was merely seconds. "So, this is the young man you were telling us about, the pilot," the Earl remarked bitterly.

"Welcome to our home," Countess Cromwell smiled, trying to subdue her husband's callousness.

"Thank you," Chase smiled nervously.

With the formal introductions over, Cassie immediately rushed them into an adjacent sitting room.

"Wow. He truly hates me."

"Chase," Cassie giggled, trying to lighten the mood. "Don't take his reactions so seriously. You're dating me, not my father. Lighten up. We still have to get through dinner."

Later that evening, after dinner's formalities were over, they went outside to the terrace's serenity.

"You survived. You weren't eaten alive," Cassie laughed, pulling Chase away from the terrace and down to the pool house. Walking inside, Cassie turned on the lights revealing a sparkling pool.

"Let's go swimming. It's heated."

"Are you crazy? What about your parents and the fact that neither of us has swimsuits."

"Chase, live in the moment. My parents will be entertaining their guests for hours, and the way my dad drinks, trust me, he'll be lucky not to pass out before he retires to his room upstairs." Quickly removing her dress and stripping down to her underwear, Cassie dove into the warm water before Chase could stop her.

"Seriously, Chase, you're just going to stand there and watch," Cassie teased, coming up for air.

Not able to take his eyes off Cassie and never having been one to sit on the sidelines, Chase quickly removed his suit. Then, wearing only black briefs, he jumped into the pool next to her.

"Geez, Cassie, you're my kind of girl. Let's just pray your dad continues to enjoy his friends and drinks as much as you suggested.

"You worry too much," Cassie laughed, grabbing hold of his muscular biceps.

Gently he pulled her towards the middle of the pool and into his arms. As their entwined bodies slowly swirled in the warm water, he kissed her.

"I love you, Cassie," Chase whispered.

"I love you too."

Although they had known each other for a short time, Cassie knew beyond a doubt that she was falling deeply in love with Chase. He was her happy place, and she loved him with every fiber of her being. She also knew that she never wanted to live without him. However, the realization that Chase was a pilot and could be transferred anywhere in the world on short notice brought tears to her eyes. Living with these concerns would be difficult. Inconspicuously, trying to wipe her face, Cassie hoped Chase wouldn't notice. However, her attempt at trying to hide her emotions failed miserably. Chase quickly sensed her worries.

"Cassie, Sweetheart, what's wrong? Have I done something to upset you?" Lovingly, Chase lifted her hands away from her face. "Oh my God, are you crying? Cassie, please, what's wrong?"

"Oh, Chase, it's just the fact I've fallen in love with you, and I'm a little emotional."

"Cassie, you know that I love you too, but I don't understand? Why are you crying?"

"Chase, you're a pilot. What if you get reassigned?" Holding onto him with every ounce of her strength, Cassie cried softly, knowing his career came with uncertainties.

"Sweetheart, is that the reason you're upset? You're worried about a reassignment?"

"Yes."

"Cassie, please don't worry. Nothing comes with guarantees. I love you." Chase knew he didn't have the answers she wanted, kissing away her tears. What she didn't realize was the fact that he shared her worries. She was right. The worst could happen. There was a war raging on the other side of the world, and the chances of his becoming involved were high. But, he was determined to remain strong enough for both of them.

"Baby, I understand your fears," Chase whispered, gently wiping her face with the back of his hand. "Trust me, do you not think I have the same worries for us. The night I first saw you changed my life forever. The circumstances surrounding our lives might be out of our control, but Sweetheart, I can promise you, you own my heart. So let's take it one day at a time and enjoy every moment we have together."

"Oh, Chase, you're right. I was the lucky one walking into the pub. I know we don't have absolute control over what happens. I think I'm just tired. It's been a long day."

"Yes. It's late. I should go. We better get out of here before someone discovers us."

"Chase, my parents have a villa in Monte Carlo. Darcy and I were planning to go down in two weeks. Could you get leave from the base and meet us there? Why don't you bring Chris? Darcy would go nuts."

"Wow, I must say you're full of surprises. Monaco," Chase paused, contemplating all the possibilities.

"Please. I promise you won't regret it."

"Cassie, any place on earth with you would be spectacular, but Monte Carlo wasn't exactly on my radar screen. I'll check the schedule at work. I can't make any promises."

"Oh, I understand your dilemma with work, but you should know your answer better be 'yes.' Honestly, I couldn't imagine being there without you."

"Sweetheart, I don't want to imagine you being there without me," Chase frowned, pulling Cassie towards the end of the pool. "Do you have any towels around here?"

"Yes. I'll grab a couple from the closet. Wait here."

She took his breath away, watching Cassie walk to the opposite end of the pool house wearing only her wet lacy underwear. After a mere glimpse of her shimmering, damp curls and sexy as hell figure, Chase knew he would move heaven and earth to join her in Monte Carlo. What guy in his right mind wouldn't?"

"Okay, here's your towel, Flyboy," Cassie teased, smacking his butt with the towel. "You better not disappoint me."

Chase pulled her close, grabbing the towel from her hand. Running his fingers through her wet hair, he savored the softness of her curls. Kissing her with intense passion, Chase could feel her petite body weaken as she melted into his.

Taking one final look at Cassie wearing only her black lace underwear, his breath hitched as he walked towards the door.

"I love you. Call me," Chase winked, leaving the pool house.

Driving back to Mildenhall, he couldn't fathom the luck of his assignment to England. He also couldn't imagine Chris's excitement when he told him about their invitation to Monte Carlo.

Chapter Five

After calling in some much-needed favors at work, a few of the guys volunteered to put in extra hours while they were gone. Chase had just enough funds tucked away to purchase their airline tickets with Chris's promise of repayment. Surprisingly, they were on their way to Monte Carlo.

Sitting in the Heathrow airport waiting to board their flight, Chris was awe-struck, contemplating their destination.

"Chase, can you believe we're on our way to Monte Carlo. How does something that unbelievable happen to a couple of young lieutenants?"

"Well, I think it's because two gorgeous young girls decided to stop at the Boar's Head for a shandy. That's the unbelievable part. It's not about the destination. Hell, Chris, I could visit Monte Carlo a thousand times, but I would be miserable if it didn't include Cassie."

"Damn, Chase, you have it bad for that girl."

"Oh, you have no idea."

"So, what do you think of Darcy?"

"She's cute. She's not typically my type, but I can hang with her for a week, especially in a Monte Carlo villa. Thankfully, my black eye healed quickly. I couldn't imagine what she might think if I showed up with the hint of a shiner.

"Well, give her a chance. You've not had the opportunity to know her. If it weren't for Darcy, my chances of ever seeing Cassie would probably have been nil. I owe that girl."

"We'll see. I'm not exactly a party pooper."

"Never said you were, Buddy. Hell, we wouldn't be roommates if you were."

"Geez, don't get all mushy on me. This conversation is going nowhere. I'm parched. I think I'll walk over and grab a soda. Do you want one?" Chris inquired, standing up to stretch his long legs.

"Yes. We don't board for another hour," Chase answered, glancing down at his watch.

Time seemed to pass at a snail's pace as Chase flipped through countless magazines. Finally, their flight was boarded and ready for take-off. In less than two hours, they would arrive in Nice, France, where Cassie and Darcy agreed to pick them up.

Arriving in Nice, the short duration of the flight had been uneventful. Chase was more than anxious to see Cassie as he grabbed his duffle bag from the overhead bin. Finally, he didn't have long to wait, making his way through a sea of people as he walked into the terminal. He recognized her voice before he saw her.

"Chase, Chase, over here," Cassie screamed, making her way through the crowd.

Chase felt like the luckiest guy on earth at the mere sight of her. Wearing her long blonde curls pulled back in a ponytail and a short red sundress, Cassie was gorgeous.

Quickly placing his duffel bag on the floor, Chase smiled. Then, with outstretched arms, he watched as Cassie ran toward him at the speed of light. Excitedly, she jumped into his arms, wrapping her legs tight around his waist. The enthusiastic affection she lavished on him made anyone watching know they were madly in love.

"I've missed you."

"Wow, Sweetheart, I've missed you too. You look incredible."

Feeling the awkwardness of the moment, Chris and Darcy laughed at seeing their friend's zealous greeting. Then, Chris broke the silence.

"Darcy, it's nice to see you again. The last time I saw you was at the Boar's Head in London," Chris smiled.

"Yes. You're right. It's nice to see you."

Picking up his duffel, Chase wrapped his arm around Cassie as they walked over to join their friends.

"So, what do you girls have planned?" he inquired.

"Well, we have a chauffeur waiting. He's going to drive us to Monte Carlo. It's less than a thirty-minute drive. Then we can either eat in once we arrive or dine out. It's your choice."

"If we eat in, who's cooking?" Chris laughed.

"Not me," Darcy quickly interjected.

"No worries. We have a chef for the duration of our stay," Cassie smiled. "Of course, if either of you feels the need to cook, the kitchen is yours."

"I vote to eat in. However, I am open to options," Chase winked wickedly, staring at Cassie.

"That's fine with me. I have no problems staying in for the night," Cassie smiled, standing on her toes to give him a quick kiss.

A stretch limo waited for them at the entrance of the airport.

"Cassie, a limo?" Chase smirked.

"Oh, I'm not complaining," Chris laughed.

Settled in for the short drive to Monte Carlo, Chase popped the cork on a Moet & Chandon Champagne bottle, filling four glasses. Finally, it appeared the party had started.

"Here's to one hell of a week in Monte Carlo," Chris toasted.

"Oh, I'll drink to that," Chase smiled, staring at Cassie.

Due to their silly antics inside the limo, the local countryside's incredible views passed unnoticed until they reached Monte Carlo. As the car neared the tiny municipality located on the beautiful shores of the Mediterranean, it made a sharp turn. Winding up the steep, narrow roads that vicariously hugged the cliff's sides, the limo slowly made its way around each hairpin turn. Lastly, entering through scrolled wrought iron gates, the car stopped in front of a two-story whitewashed stone structure. The villa wasn't massive in scale with its old-world charm, yet it showcased the other residences' specific characteristics. It appeared timeless. Tall narrow windows encased within turquoise shutters lined both levels of the structure. Their villa was almost impossible to differentiate from the others as they all shared an aged terracotta roof.

"We're here," Cassie giggled.

"Geez, Sweetheart, this place is incredible," Chase smiled.

"Thanks. I can't wait for you to see it," Cassie beamed. Then, stepping out of the limo, she grasped his hand, eagerly leading him toward the front door.

Walking inside, the ambiance of the interior didn't disappoint, with well-executed rooms leading off the foyer. Immediately, Chase was intrigued by its beauty. Intricately scrolled sconces highlighted the Venetian plastered walls and tall ceilings. Baroque furnishings exquisitely filled the entirety of the main salon.

"Come with me. You have to see the view from the terrace," Cassie grinned, pulling him through the main entrance.

A refreshing cool breeze wafted inside as Cassie opened the French doors, revealing a panoramic view of Monte Carlo. It was breathtaking. Copious rows of red-tiled villas were exquisitely tucked into the cliffs' sides and built to follow the steep terrain's natural slope. The Mediterranean's azure blue waters provided a postcard setting to the streets below, which were bustling with tourists and locals.

"Isn't it spectacular," Cassie remarked. "It's what I love most about staying here."

"Wow, it's unbelievable," Chase answered, pausing to see the phenomenal sight. No travel brochure could ever capture the natural beauty of the Mediterranean. However, as breathtaking as it appeared, Chase had only one thing on his mind, the gorgeous girl standing beside him.

"Geez, you don't see views like this every day," Chris stated, walking out with Darcy. "We're going to check out Darcy's favorite little bistro. Would you like to join us?"

Glancing at Cassie, Chase answered before he could give it a second thought.

"Why don't you go and enjoy yourselves. If it's alright with Cassie, I think we'll stay behind for the evening," Chase winked mischievously, pulling her closer.

"Yes. It's your first night in Monte Carlo. Have fun. I had Chef Andre prepare something earlier. We'll be fine," Cassie suggested.

"My kind of girl," Chase whispered.

"I have a key, so don't wait up," Darcy laughed.

"Let's go inside. We can open a bottle of wine. I'm sure Andre has something scrumptious waiting for us," Cassie suggested.

Entering the kitchen, it was small according to American standards. Yet, it had a sizeable four-burner stove and everything needed to prepare proper meals. Chase opened a bottle of wine as Cassie reached into the cabinet for glasses. Discovering a large pot of Bouillabaisse, a famous fish stew loved by the locals, still warm on the stove, and homemade bread, they were set. The evening was off to a good start, as they decided to eat outside on the terrace.

"Chase, I'm so glad you're here. I was worried that you might not be able to get away from the base," Cassie frowned, taking a sip of wine.

"Trust me, I was worried too, but Chris and I got lucky. We called in a few favors, and it worked. By the way, do your parents know that Chris and I came down for the week?"

"Only my mom, and she was entirely on board. However, my dad doesn't. What he doesn't know won't hurt him," Cassie laughed, pouring herself another glass of wine.

"What do you and Darcy normally do when staying at the Villa?"

"Well, for starters, we like to sunbathe. We don't get a lot of sunshine back home or warm weather. Darcy is a social butterfly. She loves the casinos and eating at her favorite cafes."

"What do you like?" Chase inquired, setting their empty dishes aside as he pulled Cassie into his lap.

"I like the fact that you're here," Cassie teased with a whisper, lovingly running her fingers through his hair. "I've told you, not a lot impresses me."

"Geez, Cassie, that's sad. Monte Carlo is unbelievable and offers so many things to do. I think it's time to change your perspective, and this week will be the perfect time to create some new memories. So maybe we should get started on those," Chase winked.

"Maybe we should," Cassie giggled playfully. "Let's go inside."

In only a matter of minutes, their clothes lay scattered across the floor of the primary suite. Wrapped in Chase's muscular arms, Cassie felt loved. It didn't take exotic locations, things, or money to make her happy, only the handsome guy lying next to her.

Reaching over to turn off the light, Chase was determined to ensure Cassie would have new memories of being in Monte Carlo. Memories that would carry her for a lifetime.

Later that night, Chris and Darcy returned from an evening of food, fun, and too much drinking. "Wow, it's quiet," Darcy laughed, quickly tossing her shoes in the corner.

"Yes, too quiet. Do you think they decided to go out?"

"Are you kidding? Those two? They were lucky to make it upstairs to the primary suite before they ripped their clothes off," Darcy laughed. "That leaves one bedroom upstairs and one downstairs. I'm upstairs. You can take the one downstairs at the end of the hall. It has an ensuite, and you should find everything you need. Thanks for a fun evening. I'll see you in the morning," Darcy mentioned, running up the stairs and leaving Chris on his own.

Cassie was the first to wake up the following day as sunlight slowly crept underneath the heavy brocade drapes. Staring at the sexy young man in her bed, she knew she never wanted to be without him. Thoughts of their future together and the random fact that he could get orders to Vietnam brought a tear to her eyes. Trying hard not to get emotional and purging the thoughts from her mind, she promised to live in the moment. They had today, and she didn't want to waste another moment. Smothering Chase with smooches, he slowly opened his eyes.

"Wow, Sweetheart, you look incredible," Chase smiled, pulling her into his arms, and returning her gentle kisses.

"Chase, I have bed hair, and I'm sure morning breath. How is that even remotely possible?"

"Babe, you're silly. I love how you look in the morning, especially after last night. You're gorgeous, and I couldn't love you more," Chase smiled, slowly waking up.

Taking their kisses deeper, Cassie wasn't ready to leave the comfort of being held in his arms.

"Sweetheart, if you continue, we won't be going anywhere," Chase softly whispered. He knew their time together was tenuous at best, and if she needed him, breakfast could wait, Darcy and Chris could wait, hell, Monte Carlo could wait. Pulling her closer, they simply shut out the world. Loving Cassie felt natural, as if they had known each other for a hundred lifetimes.

Finally, Cassie smiled, coming up for air, staring into his eyes. "Geez, do we have to get out of bed?"

"I'm afraid we must, or I fear they will eventually find our shriveled bodies."

"Oh, that's funny," Cassie snickered. "Race you to the shower."

Getting dressed, they were ready to take the 'walk of shame' downstairs and endure all the snide remarks, which inevitably Chris and Darcy would hurl at them.

"Wow, you're alive," Darcy complained. "Geez, Cassie, the day is half gone, and you do realize we're in Monte Carlo, right?"

"Jealous?" Cassie vented, walking past Darcy on her way to the kitchen.

"Yeah, we were almost thinking of heading down to the beach without you," Chris scoffed, taking a sip of coffee.

"Buddy, please tell me there's more hot coffee," Chase laughed.

After finishing breakfast, which Chef Andre had kept warm, and several cups of coffee, they were finally ready to enjoy a day at the beach.

"Why don't we rent Vespas?" Cassie suggested.

At the very hint of renting Vespa scooters, it appeared they were immediately back in the good graces of their friends. Packing a picnic lunch, which included wine, they were all set to start their Monte Carlo adventures. Waiting outside for their driver to take them to the nearest rental, Cassie quickly pulled her hair into a ponytail. The girls were dressed to enjoy a day of sunbathing, wearing bikinis under their crochet swimsuit covers.

Arriving at the rental shop, they rented two Vespas. The guys agreed to drive. Cassie hopped on a red Vespas behind Chase, storing their packed lunch, and Darcy rode behind Chris on a matching blue model. Chase and Chris had no idea of the direction they were heading or the location.

"Do you girls have any idea where we're going?" Chase questioned.

"Of course," they both eagerly chimed in. "Just follow the coastline until we're out of town, and not much farther is a private cove. It's our favorite place to swim and sunbathe," Darcy added.

"Usually, there's no one there. Only the locals know about this secluded spot. So let's go, Flyboy," Cassie laughed.

Monte Carlo was visually stunning, passing numerous quaint shops and outdoor restaurants beautifully accessorized with tables shaded by blue cobalt umbrellas. Soon they were away from the congested traffic, which slowly snarled along the harbor. Speeding along the narrow coastal highway, which hugged the azure blue waters of the Mediterranean on one side and near-vertical cliffs on the other, the warmth of the sun and the cool breeze felt exhilarating.

"Turn right here," Cassie yelled loudly.

Checking the rearview mirror, Chris and Darcy appeared behind them as they turned onto a short sandy road. The location was perfect. Parking the Vespas, they looked forward to soaking up the sun and enjoying the warm, clear turquoise water.

"Awesome. We're the only ones here," Cassie announced, grabbing the picnic supplies.

Chase grasped Cassie's hand as they sprinted towards the beach, leaving Darcy to spread out two large blankets and uncork the wine. It seemed the fun had started. Watching as Cassie removed her swimsuit cover, Chase was speechless. Trying hard to remain in control at the mere sight of Cassie wearing a black thong bikini was killing him. Once again, she had no idea her effect on him. He might fly F-4 Phantoms, but one look at her, and he could easily forget his name. She simply took his breath away. Wasting no time, Chase stripped down to his swim trunks. Scooping Cassis into his arms, he carried her down to the water's edge. Clinging to his back and shoulders, Cassie held tightly to him as he slowly took her further into the warm water. Suddenly, a wave caught them off guard, taking them under with its force. Coming up for air, Cassie gasped. Wiping her eyes as she pulled her hair away from her face, Chase quickly pulled them upright.

"Geez, Chase, are you trying to drown me."

"Sweetheart, I think we both went under," Chase laughed. "Maybe this will help." His lips met hers with intensity as he pulled her into the safety of his arms.

"Hey," Chris yelled. "You guys can't remain upright even in the Mediterranean," he added, roaring with laughter as he walked into the water.

"Yeah, I think you guys are better suited for a kiddie pool," Darcy laughed, splashing through the oncoming waves behind Chris.

After an hour of playfully enjoying the warm sparkling water, it seemed to spark their appetites.

"Is anyone hungry? We have gourmet sandwiches and plenty of wine. Compliments of our chef," Cassie announced.

"You don't have to ask me twice," Chris answered, getting out of the water. "I'm starved."

Chase poured everyone a glass of wine as Cassie passed out sandwiches piled high with ham, turkey, and cheese. Along with a host of condiments and veggies, their day at the beach had now become an epicurean adventure.

"Wow, this is the life," Chris smiled, taking a sip of wine.

"Cassie and I love spending time here," Darcy mentioned. "Tomorrow night, I'll take you to my favorite casino."

"Oh, I'm sure Chris will love that. Unfortunately, however, I'm not so confident about his card skills. So I usually wind up taking his money," Chase laughed.

"Really, speak for yourself," Chris snapped.

After consuming their sandwiches and drinking several glasses of wine, Chase felt incredibly relaxed. Lying down on the blanket, he gently pulled Cassie down beside him. Temporarily falling asleep with Cassie snuggled into his arms, they lost track of time as the sun slowly began to set. The winds shifted a few hours later, becoming more robust and cooler. Finally, Darcy knew it was time to leave.

"Hey, you sleeping, love birds. It's getting late. We should go," Darcy said softly.

Oh, I think we should leave without them," Chris teased. "After all, they thought nothing of making us wait this morning."

"That's not happening, even though I agree it would be funny," Darcy laughed, reaching over to wake Cassie.

"Cassie, sorry it's late. Chris and I are going back to the villa. Thought you should know."

"I'll wake Chase. Wait up. We're coming," Cassie replied.

Slowly, Chase turned towards Cassie, opening his eyes, holding her down in jest as he playfully kissed her.

"Geez, lieutenant, get a room," Chris laughed. "Oh, that's right, you have one back at the villa."

"Knock it off, Chris, or I'll make sure Mad Dog sits behind you every time you fly those friendly skies."

"Yeah, well, that will never happen," Chris grimaced.

After packing up, they decided to drive straight back to the villa. The Vespas were rented for the remainder of the week, allowing them to enjoy the sights of Monte Carlo at their leisure.

Arriving back at the villa, Darcy and Chris decided to go out for drinks, leaving Cassie and Chase alone for the evening.

"Don't wait up," Chris yelled before leaving.

"Not a chance," Chase responded boisterously from upstairs.

Stepping out of the shower, Cassie wrapped her hair in a white terrycloth turban. Walking over to where Chase sat, thumbing through a brochure that advertised local boat tours and offered snorkeling, she curled up on his lap. "So Flyboy, is that something you're interested in?" she whispered.

"Maybe?"

"Well, we can put that on our to-do list if you want to check it out. Do you feel like cooking? I'm craving a juicy steak?" Cassie questioned, changing the subject.

"You're in luck. Steaks are my specialty," Chase winked.

"Really, well, I'll be the judge of that. Let's go downstairs."

Entering the kitchen, Chase found everything he needed to satisfy Cassie's craving. It wasn't long before he had the entire villa infused with the savory aroma of pan-seared steaks, grilled onions, and mushrooms. Hurriedly adding a couple of side dishes to impress her further, Chase opened a bottle of wine. Dining outside on the terrace under an array of twinkling stars, Cassie felt it was one of the most romantic meals she had ever eaten.

"Geez, Chase, I swear this steak is incredible. You're a genius in the kitchen," Cassie smiled, enjoying the last morsel. "I'm stuffed."

"I'm glad you approve," Chase smiled with a wink as he removed their plates back to the kitchen. Then, returning with another bottle of wine, he refilled their glasses.

"Today has been perfect," Cassie mentioned, dragging her wrought-iron chaise lounge closer to his.

"Sweetheart, come here," Chase grinned, pulling her into his lap as he gently removed the turban, which still covered her hair. Then, he tenderly caressed her face, running his fingers through her loose blonde curls. "You're right. Today was perfect," he whispered, kissing her softly.

Laying her head on his shoulders, the relaxing effect of the wine took control of her body. Cassie was quickly losing her fight to remain awake. Within a few short minutes, she succumbed as sleep invaded her petite body. Gently lifting her in his arms, he carried her upstairs and placed her beneath the warm covers. Removing his clothes, he slipped into bed next to her. Starring at the love of his life, she slept peacefully. Chase knew that whatever their future held, hopefully, the memories they made this week would carry them for a lifetime.

Unexpectedly waking in the middle of the night, Cassie felt the warm embrace of Chase's body wrapped around her. Opening her eyes, she smiled, realizing that he was a true gentleman. He had carried her to bed, only removing her shoes. Trying not to wake him, she softly kissed his lips. Suddenly, his gentle hands caressed her face bringing her lips back to his. "Let's get you out of these clothes," he whispered. The wee hours of the morning quickly shifted from sleep to ecstasy.

Waking as the mid-day sun blissfully brightened every corner of the bedroom, it appeared they had overslept. Glancing at the time, 1:45 p.m., it reflected what they already suspected.

"Geez, it's late," Cassie giggled, returning from the bathroom. "It's unbelievably quiet. I think Darcy and Chris may have taken one of the Vespas and left us behind."

"Can't say that I would blame them. We've overslept?" Chase mentioned as he sat up in bed, rubbing his growth of dark stubble.

"Well, if you hadn't kept me awake," Cassie grinned, tossing a large decorative pillow toward him.

Catching it before it hit the headboard, Chase laughed. "Sweetheart, I believe you were the one who instigated us being awake," he smiled wickedly.

"Maybe," Cassie snickered. "I'll let you explain that to Darcy."

"Really," Chase laughed. "Darcy isn't a child. But, somehow, I think she might understand."

Cassie pulled him out of bed and toward the shower like two kids at play. Then, dressing casually for the day, unsure of their plans, they headed downstairs to make coffee.

There was no sign of Darcy or Chris. Checking the Vespas, Chase laughed.

"You were right on the Vespas. They're both gone. I'm sure it's a subtle hint. Probably Chris's idea."

Finding a note on the kitchen island, Cassie read it aloud.

"Figured you wouldn't have any need for the Vespas, as you can't even get out of bed. Be dressed by 7:00 p.m. Dinner reservations for four. Formal."

"It appears we have dinner reservations this evening. Knowing Darcy, it's probably at one of the more elegant restaurants located inside her favorite casino. Did you bring a suit?"

"A suit. You must be joking. The only suits that Chris and I wear these days are flight suits. It looks as if we'll be staying in for the night. Think you could handle it, sweetheart," Chase teased playfully.

"Oh, Lieutenant Morgan, don't get any ideas. We're going. One phone call and I'll arrange everything. I'll have suits and accessories brought up to the villa. I just need sizes. No worries."

With her influence and financial standing, Cassie could easily arrange anything at a moment's notice.

Later that afternoon, Darcy and Chris arrived back at the villa. It appeared they had spent the entire day playing the role of tourists. Soon afterward, the suits arrived. The only thing remaining was to be dressed before the limo came.

Helping Chase with his tie, the mere sight of him took her breath away. The black designer suit seamlessly molded to his tall, muscular frame. With his chiseled facial features, jet black hair, and dreamy blue eyes, she knew she would be the envy of every girl who laid eyes on him. Cassie couldn't wait to be seen on his arm at dinner and later at the casino.

Walking downstairs, wearing her blonde hair swept back with a diamond clasp, Cassie, without doubt, was glowing. A silk backless blush gown accented her curves, and matching Italian stilettos, completed her ensemble.

"Wow," Chris remarked, watching as Cassie slowly descended the stairs with her arm around Chase. "The car is here. Is everyone ready?"

Walking outside, Chris took Darcy's hand. Towering over her, he was statuesque and handsome. Darcy's flowing emerald chiffon gown complemented her red hair, which she wore in loose curls. "You look exquisite," Chris grinned.

Helping the girls inside the limo, they were about to experience the nightlife of Monte Carlo, which undoubtedly was in a league of its own.

Arriving at the Casino de Monte-Carlo, it was palatial. The grandeur of the world-famous casino and hotel was beyond anything that Chase and Chris had ever experienced. Entering the casino, Darcey was eager to become their tour guide as she pointed out its massive architectural design. Tall columns extended upward into the ornate gold ceilings. The degree of gilded gold opulence, sculptures, and large crystal chandeliers was unparalleled.

"Wow, talk about a fish out of water," Chris laughed.

"Yes. This is a little above our pay grade," Chase whispered.

Cassie laughed. "Geez, I think you're both being silly. Let's eat."

After dining in one of the casino's well-known restaurants, Café de Paris, it was time for a bit of fun.

Trying to hold Chris back from emptying his wallet at one of the gaming tables wasn't going to be an easy feat.

"Buddy, give me your wallet," Chase laughed, knowing Chris's record with card games wasn't exactly in his favor.

Taking a seat at a nearby Black Jack table, they watched with bated breath as Chris picked up his cards. Receiving his next card, Chris hit a perfect twenty-one. Watching as Chris flaunted his win, they feared it was only beginner's luck. Unfortunately, it only confirmed their suspicions as the cards were not in his favor as the game continued. Deciding to walk away appeared to be a wise decision.

"Sorry, Buddy," Chase frowned, playfully slapping Chris on his back.

"Let's try the roulette tables," Darcy giggled.

"I'm not sure the odds are better," Cassie smirked.

Making their way through the casino toward the Roulette tables, Cassie and Chase laughed. However, they were determined to support their friends, knowing the odds were not in their favor.

"Geez, Cassie, it's a casino. Lighten up. I think you and Chase have forgotten how to have fun," Darcy smirked.

"Oh, I think that's debatable," Chase winked playfully, pulling Cassie closer.

Deciding not to be outdone by her best friend, Cassie found a roulette table with a high max bet and a small minimum. Watching as Chris and Darcy placed their bets, Cassie also placed a bet. Unfortunately, as the wheel slowly stopped, it quickly appeared no one had won. Deciding to place a double street bet, Cassie crossed her fingers. Squeezing Chase's hand, Cassie held her breath. Then, as the wheel slowly came to a stop, she screamed. Unbelievably, she won.

"Wow, Sweetheart, guess you showed them."

Deciding to leave Chris and Darcy at the roulette table, Cassie and Chase walked over to a side lounge to enjoy a few drinks. After an hour, the unlucky duo approached with sad faces.

"What happened?" Cassie laughed. "Not having any fun?"

Darcy frowned. "Let's just say we're ready to call it a night."

"Yes. We should go," Chris added.

"Geez, Buddy, I hope you didn't drop your whole month's pay. Rent is due when we get back to Mildenhall."

"No comment," Chris scowled.

"Well, that's a definite. We're out of here," Chase grimaced.

Entering the limo for the short ride, Cassie was again a victim of overindulgence after consuming three glasses. Once again, falling asleep in Chase's arms, he smiled, knowing she was a lightweight where alcohol was concerned.

Arriving at the villa, he carried Cassie upstairs as Chris and Darcy decided to retire for the evening. Carefully removing her shoes, he gently laid her under the covers. Unable to sleep, Chase found himself in a quandary of emotions staring at the gorgeous young girl whose long blonde curls effortlessly flowed over her pillow. Desperately needing a cigarette, he reached into his duffle bag. Deciding to have a quick smoke outside on the terrace, Chase stopped in the kitchen for a bottle of wine. Then he walked out, quietly popping the cork on a bottle and grabbing a glass. Setting the bottle and glass down on a nearby table, he lounged back in one of the wrought iron chairs. Removing his tie and unbuttoning the top buttons on his dress shirt, Chase cupped his hand against the chilly evening breeze, lighting a cigarette. Thoughts of Cassie consumed him as he took a sip of wine. For the first time since they met, Chase contemplated his decisions. Was it selfish of him to want her, need her, love her if he couldn't guarantee their future? Thoughts of his career, the war raging in Vietnam, and the contemplation of hurting her killed him. It would be better that they had never met than to cause her pain. Pouring another glass of wine, he no longer wanted to be sober.

Suddenly, he felt loving, tender hands caressing his tense shoulders.

"Is it a private party, or may I join you?" Cassie whispered.

"Sweetheart, I thought you were asleep."

"I was until I discovered your side of the bed was cold, and I realized you were gone. You know it's impossible to sleep without you," Cassie frowned. "Is everything alright? You seem worried. Are you sure you're okay?"

"I'm fine," Chase smiled, pulling her into his lap. "I couldn't sleep, and I didn't want to wake you, so I decided to have a cigarette and a glass of wine."

"Well, lieutenant, next time, wake me, and I'll join you," Cassie smiled demurely. Then, she delicately covered his face with kisses, running her fingers through his hair.

Caressing her face, he brought her lips down to meet his, kissing her with extreme desire. Feeling heat radiate throughout her body, Cassie felt as though her body was melting into his like molten wax. "Let's take this party upstairs," he whispered breathlessly.

"My thoughts exactly," Cassie agreed as he carried her inside.

For the remainder of the evening and early morning, sleep was a non-issue.

The following days, they didn't miss anything on their list. Cassie reserved a boat which took them snorkeling in the clear cobalt waters. They dined in the best restaurants, and the guys waited as the girls shopped tirelessly. Then, all too soon, their time together in Monte Carlo came to an end. It was the day of their departure.

Kissing Cassie goodbye at the airport, Chase knew that regardless if time wasn't on their side, he was determined to make the most of every second they had. He would see her the following week.

Chapter Six

Waking up the following morning in the small row house in Mildenhall, the past week felt surreal. It seemed unbelievable that two young lieutenants who had been in England less than two months had already enjoyed the best that Monte Carlo had to offer. It was time to face the week ahead, which meant dealing with the guys at work.

Bounding down the stairs, Chris yelled. "Let's go. We can't afford to be late this morning. After all the favors we called in, they'll have our heads on a platter."

"And whose fault is that?"

"Sorry, Dude, the alarm didn't go off."

"Well, maybe it's time you invested in a new clock."

Arriving at the base, Chase gave Chris a stern warning glance before they walked into the squadron. Having threatened Chris the night before to keep the details of their trip off the record, it was time to see if he could finally keep his word. So, encountering Mad Dog, who was back from his TDY, it began.

"Well, if it isn't the boys from Monte Carlo," Mad Dog roared.

"Yeah, what was that like, I mean, frigging hell, Monte Carlo?" Lieutenant Stevenson yelled from across the room.

"No comment," Chris reacted.

"Oh, did Chase threaten that pretty face of yours again if you talked?" Mad Dog laughed.

"Back off. You, slimeballs, will never be fortunate enough to have that experience," Chase vented, reaching for his helmet. "Let's go, Mad Dog. There's a phantom on the tarmac with our names on it."

Later that afternoon, while tossing back a few drinks at the Officer's Club, it was apparent they were no longer the topic of discussion. Unfortunately, one of the young lieutenants had made the costly mistake of getting a DUI, driving under the influence. His misfortune was now their reprieve.

With the coming weekend, Cassie consumed Chase's thoughts. Their few phone calls during the week were not enough. He had to see her. Without his knowledge, Cassie shared his thoughts and made arrangements to surprise him. A soft knock at the door would change his weekend.

"Oh my God," Chris reacted, opening the door. "Does Chase know you were coming over, and what's with the black hair?"

"No. Do you like it? I wanted to surprise Chase. Is he here?"

"Yes, come in. I almost didn't recognize you."

"It's a wig, silly. George dropped me off."

"Well, then, don't let me stop you. Chase is upstairs."

Quietly making her way up the narrow stairs to Chase's room, he was in the shower. Wearing the wig, Cassie nervously sat on the edge of the bed. Trying hard to keep her composure and refrain from giggling like a mindless teenager, she couldn't wait to surprise him. Suddenly as the bathroom door opened, Chase walked out with only a towel wrapped around his incredibly sexy physique. The mere sight of him sent shivers of excitement racing throughout her petite body. His reaction was priceless, making it worth every lie she had to tell her parents.

"Oh my God," Chase gasped. "Wow, Sweetheart, you look sexy with black hair. You certainly know how to make a man's day," he smiled mischievously, pulling her into his arms. Then, holding her against his buffed, bare chest, they consumed each other with lavish enthusiastic kisses.

Inhaling the fragrance of Cassie's perfume, Chase smiled. "Sweetheart, I love the wig. Maybe you should keep it," he whispered, kissing the nape of her neck.

"So, what's the plan? How long do you have?"

"Oh, only a couple of hours. My parents think I'm shopping with Darcy."

"Well, we're not wasting a minute. Wait here."

Running downstairs, Chase threw the car keys at Chris, who was lounging back on the sofa watching a British game show.

"Hey, man, do you mind? I need a few hours with Cassie."

"You're going to owe me. I'll drive out to the base and work out for a few hours."

"Whatever. I always owe you."

Quickly running up the stairs, he couldn't wait to be alone with the mysterious girl wearing the black wig.

"Chris is leaving. We have the place to ourselves," Chase winked with a smile.

"Oh, I hope he doesn't mind."

"Sweetheart, it's not a threesome," Chase teased wickedly, loosening his towel as it slowly fell away. He slowly sauntered toward her. "Now, let's get you out of these clothes."

"Wow, Flyboy, you don't waste any time," Cassie laughed.

"Why should we waste time?" Chase whispered, gently unbuttoning her blouse. "God, I've missed you."

Making love like two crazy teenagers on a first date, they spent the entire afternoon in bed, barely coming up for air. Cassie had taken possession of his heart the first time he saw her. He couldn't imagine his life without her. Knowing that she wouldn't be staying overnight and the thought of her leaving, it frantically sent him in search of a cigarette. Rolling over, he reached for his pack sitting on the nightstand. Lighting a smoke, he lounged back against the headboard, pulling Cassie closer. He had the only thing he ever wanted in his arms.

"Are you hungry?" Chase questioned.

"Famished."

"Why don't we jump in the shower, get dressed, and I'll make blueberry pancakes and bacon.

"Sounds scrumptious. But, remember, I don't cook."

"No worries. I've got this."

Taking Cassie's hand, he led her into the bathroom. Standing under the warm water as it washed over them, he envisioned what life would be like with Cassie. After their fantastic week in Monte Carlo, she was the first thought he had in the morning and the last at night.

"Shampoo?" Chase laughed, lathering her hair with a soft fragrance.

Towering over her, he stooped gently so she could massage his hair with her fingers. Slowly, Cassie rubbed his firm muscular torso with body wash. Hesitating, she looked up. Confused by her hesitation, he grasped her petite hands. Holding them in his, he guided her soft hands tenderly across his abs.

"Sweetheart, it's okay. I'm all yours. I love you," Chase smiled, softly kissing the nape of her neck.

Cassie knew life without Chase was no longer an option. But, first, she had to convince her parents that he was *the one.* Perhaps, with time, her father would change his mind regarding Americans, specifically Chase.

Stepping out of the shower, Cassie wrapped her damp hair in a towel. Then, getting dressed, they hurried downstairs to the kitchen.

Finding all the ingredients to make blueberry pancakes, it wasn't long before the kitchen took on the aroma of pancakes and fried bacon. Deciding coffee was the only missing element, Chase plugged in the electric kettle.

Setting the table, she knew life with Chase might entail the loss of her pampered lifestyle. However, catching a glimpse of Chase's sexy physique flipping pancakes, she felt like the luckiest girl in the world. Walking into the Boar's Head that evening had changed her life forever, and she wouldn't go back and change a thing.

Finishing her last piece of bacon, Cassie glanced up, noting the time on the clock in the kitchen.

"I've got to go. George will be here in a few minutes," she panicked.

Hurriedly running upstairs, she removed the towel covering her hair. She brushed out her long blonde curls and looked around the bedroom for anything she might be leaving behind. Finally, walking out to the front door, she turned around.

"When will I see you?" Chase asked.

"I'll call you. Maybe I can get away next week."

After one last kiss, Chase watched as Cassie walked out the door and entered the black hackney carriage. Then, remembering the mess he had created earlier, he walked back into the kitchen to clean up. Just as he was drying the last plate, he heard the front door open.

"Honey, I'm home," Chris yelled.

The aroma of fried bacon led him straight into the kitchen.

"Well, how did it go this afternoon," Chris questioned, walking over to the stove and searching for leftovers.

"Oh, you have no idea."

"Awesome. Any leftovers?"

"You're lucky. I just put extra pancakes and bacon in the fridge."

"Any plans for tomorrow?"

"No. Cassie was lucky to get away today. She told her parents she was shopping with Darcy."

"Hey, do we still have that bottle of Jamesons?"

"Yeah."

"Well, grab a couple of glasses and bring the bottle into the living room. We have to talk. I heard some rumors today at the gym. Trust me. You're going to need something strong."

Reaching for the whiskey and glasses, Chase knew the news wasn't good. He could only pray that Chris wouldn't confirm his worst fear. Then, walking into the living room, he opened the bottle and poured them each a drink.

"Thanks, man."

Quickly tossing back his drink, Chris reached for the bottle. "Rumors have it that Mad Dog got orders," Chris stated, pouring another drink.

"And, that's a bad thing?" Chase laughed. "I'll finally get a new wizzo."

"Buddy, that's not all. Rumors are more orders are coming?"

"Is this a joke?" Chase scowled, rubbing his forehead as he downed his remaining drink and then poured another.

"Sorry, I wouldn't joke about something like this," Chris frowned, taking a long slow sip.

"Oh, my God," Chase grimaced. "Cassie."

"I know, man, I know."

Chase no longer wanted to be sober, grabbing the bottle away from Chris.

"Hey, go easy on that. Nothing official has reached us yet. But, hell, we might get lucky."

Reaching for a pack of Marlboro, Chase lit a cigarette.

"Can I bum one of those?"

"Sure."

Lounging back on the sofa, Chris felt terrible for Chase. He hated being the bearer of bad news. However, his source was reliable. Graduating from the Air Force Academy and flying F-4s, they were prime candidates to enter the war. England was simply a pit stop for training. Putting out his cigarette, Chris was ready to call it a night.

"I'm turning in for the evening. I think you should call it a night."

"Really, you think I can sleep. Hell, get upstairs."

"Chase, I feel your pain, but don't kill the messenger. Remember, we haven't received any news yet."

Chris knew there was nothing he could do for Chase. So leaving his buddy to drink alone and deal with his thoughts was the best he could do for a friend.

Lifting the bottle of Jameson to his mouth, Chase had no further need for a glass. It was going to be a long night. Lighting another cigarette, thoughts of Cassie consumed him. One thing he knew for sure, he would not mention a word of this to her. Chris was right, they had not received orders, and until they did, it would never be open for discussion. Laying his head back against the sofa, thoughts of home and his mother came to mind. If and when the time came that he would have to give her news of orders to Vietnam, he knew she would be devastated. Being the only son certainly didn't help. Downing the last of the Jameson, he finally fell asleep.

Chapter Seven

Another month passed with no further hint of assignments in their squadron. Chase was relieved yet determined to spend every possible moment with Cassie. Then, late one evening, she called with a shocking invitation. It was an official invite to dinner with her parents and not one he could easily turn down. However, it gave him an ominous feeling, like being chosen to stand in front of a firing squad. The following Saturday, George arrived to pick him up.

"Good evening, sir," George smiled, opening the car door.

"Good evening, George," Chase replied nervously, entering the back seat.

"I believe the Earl is expecting you to arrive by 7:00 p.m. It's a short drive, and I should have you there right on time," George stated, closing the car door.

"Thanks, George."

Arriving at the manor house, Cassie greeted him at the front door.

"You look nervous."

"I don't think nervous covers it."

"Don't be silly. You'll be fine," Cassie laughed, taking his hand. "Remember, it's not formal. Just relax."

Cassie led Chase into a well-appointed room adjacent to the formal dining room. They waited for her parents to make their appearance. Afterward, everyone would be seated for dinner. They didn't have long to wait as the Earl, and Countess of Cromwell walked in.

"Awe," Earl Cromwell paused, giving Chase a somewhat intimidating stare. "The young American pilot," he stated in a harsh tone.

"Thank you for coming," the Countess graciously acknowledged.

Following behind Cassie, they were seated across from her parents. As the staff served the first course, the continued stares from the Earl made Chase feel anxious. Then, before he could lift his glass, the rude comments began.

"My sister married an American, and I must say it didn't bode well for the family. He was self-centered, egotistical, and not a very likable gent," Earl Cromwell spoke up, not once taking his eyes off Chase.

"Ian, I believe they were well suited," the Countess countered.

"Yes. I believe Aunt Olivia was very much in love," Cassie added, trying to lighten the conversation.

"Well, be that as it may, I find most Americans to be offensive by nature," Earl Cromwell continued. "Unfortunately, my sister made the unwise decision to follow him to the states, relinquishing her title. Frankly, I've never forgiven her for her foolish choices."

"Dear, I don't believe our guest should be subjected to your narrow-minded opinions."

As the evening progressed and everyone finished with dinner, Earl Cromwell had easily managed to make his hatred for Americans very apparent.

"Thank you for dinner," Chase stated, trying to force a smile.

"Please excuse us," Cassie said.

Pulling back Cassie's chair, Chase grasped her hand as they left the dining room. Cassie's mother followed them out.

"Cassie, dear, why don't you invite your young American pilot for a weekend at our home on the Isle of Wight. I'll call the staff and have them prepare for your arrival. I'm sure he would love to see more of our beautiful country."

"Thanks, Mom, and he does have a name," Cassie vented. "It's Chase."

Hurriedly, Cassie led Chase out of the main house and down to the pool house.

"Oh my God," Cassie yelled, turning on the lights as they entered. "Chase, I'm so sorry. I never thought they would be that vindictive. Can you ever forgive me?" she cried.

"Cassie, listen, with all honesty, nothing surprised me. Don't be so hard on yourself. It's not your parents that I've fallen in love with. It's you. However," Chase paused. "I would love to visit the Isle of Wight. I think it was a genuine invitation from your mom to make up for your dad's hostilities. I like her tenacity and how she spoke up to counter his disdain for Americans."

"Oh, Chase, no wonder I fell in love with you," Cassie cried, putting her arms around him.

"No more tears," Chase smiled, wiping her moist cheeks with the back of his hand. "I love you."

"Oh, Flyboy, I love you too, even if you are an American pilot," she snickered.

"That's my girl," he winked. "Cassie, it's late, and I should get back."

"What? We're not swimming?"

"Seriously," Chase laughed. "The last thing we need is your father to discover us in the pool house. I'm sure he would shoot me on sight."

Pulling Cassie closer into his arms, he inhaled the delicate scent of her hair. Then, Chase gently drew her lips to his, caressing her face and kissing her softly. "I love you. Walk with me out to the car."

Putting his arm around her waist, they safely made it back to the main house without encountering her parents. Watching as George opened the car door, Chase quickly kissed her goodbye. "Oh, I can't wait to see you wearing your sexy black string bikini when we visit the Isle of Wight," he winked.

"For your eyes only, Lieutenant Morgan," Cassie blushed.

Arriving back at the row house in Mildenhall, Chris was up late watching television and enjoying a New Castle Brown Ale.

"So, how did that go?" Chris inquired.

"Well, there's no doubt Cassie's father hates Americans. Darcy nailed it when she said he hates Yanks."

"I'm sorry. Sounds like a rough evening," Chris frowned.

"Yes, for the most part. However, it ended on a more positive note. Cassie's mother, Jaclyn, or I should say the Countess of Cromwell, has invited me to the Isle of Wight. They have a summer home on the island. I think she was trying to save face after her husband's derogatory remarks during dinner."

"Wow, Monte Carlo and now the Isle of Wight. Let's hope that Captain Whitman gives you leave."

"Oh, it'll just be over the weekend. I can't take any more leave this soon."

"Would you like a New Castle?" Chris asked, making his way into the kitchen.

"No, thanks. I'm going upstairs to bed. It was tiring listening to Cassie's father spew out his hatred towards Americans."

"I'm surprised you didn't call him out," Chris laughed, walking back into the living room with another ale.

"What would have been the point? He's a bitter old man, even if he does have a title in front of his name. I felt terrible for Cassie."

"You're a good man, Charlie Brown."

"See you in the morning," Chase laughed, going upstairs.

Getting into bed, thoughts of seeing Cassie in her sexy black bikini made the entire evening worthwhile. Soon they would be visiting the Isle of Wight.

Chapter Eight

Leaving the base earlier than usual for a Friday evening, they were off duty. Only hours away from seeing Cassie, Chase couldn't believe his fortune to be spending another weekend with her. Compliments no less to her mother, whose opinions of Americans thankfully didn't reflect those of her husband, the Earl of Cambridge.

"Geez, Chase, I can't believe you're off to the Isle of Wight while I sit at home and twiddle my thumbs."

"Well, believe it. You'll have the place all to yourself."

"Let's swing by the Class Six Store. I need to pick up a few supplies," Chris scowled.

After making a quick stop for beer and snacks, they arrived home. Turning on the telly, Chris opened a bottle of New Castle and lounged back on the sofa. Lucky for him, he would have a marathon of British Game Shows to keep him company.

Grabbing a cold beer from the fridge, Chase ran upstairs to pack what few things he would need. The image of Cassie wearing her black thong bikini consumed him. In less than an hour, he would once again hold the only thing in life that mattered to him.

Hearing a light knock at the door, Chris pulled himself up from the sofa.

"Hey, Cassie, come in. You're early. He's upstairs."

Hearing the sound of her voice, Chase bounded down the stairs. "Sweetheart, you look amazing."

"Thanks. If you're ready, George is waiting. Chris, have a nice weekend," Cassie remarked. "Oh, I almost forgot. Darcy said to give her a ring at her flat if you got bored. She mentioned something about you going with her to Hunstanton Beach."

"Thanks," Chris replied, sporting a huge smile.

"Good evening, Sir," George stated, opening the car door.

"Good evening, George."

"What? No, Limo?" Chase teased, getting inside the car after Cassie.

"George is merely dropping us at the airport. Mom talked my father into letting us use the Cessna, and Frank will fly us down. He's a good friend of my father, and I didn't want to waste a moment of our time."

"Geez, Sweetheart, you're my kind of girl. Flying is the only way to travel," Chase whispered, pulling her into his arms.

Upon their arrival at the Sandown Airport on the Isle of Wight, an older distinguished gentleman met them as they departed the aircraft.

"Good evening, Lady Cromwell. I hope your flight was enjoyable."

"Yes, James, thanks for asking," Cassie smiled. "James, Lieutenant Morgan will be joining me for the weekend."

"Good evening, sir. I'll take your luggage."

"Thanks, but that won't be necessary. I only have a carry-on bag."

Chase wasn't sure what to expect entering the car for the short ride to Brightstone Bay. However, after visiting the manor house in Cambridge and staying at the villa in Monte Carlo, he was confident he would not be disappointed. The expansive Jacobean manor house was breathtaking, surrounded by its impressive manicured grounds. Yet, the grandeur of the two-story stone structure appeared formidable.

"Wow, this is where you spent your summers?" Chase inquired, totally mesmerized by the sprawling structure.

"Yes, but I've always been partial to spending summers at our villa in Monte Carlo. But, of course, Mom always preferred Brightstone. Tomorrow, I'll give you the grand tour, but right now, I'm starved."

Exiting the car, Cassie took his hand. Entering the estate through the kitchen, the aroma of fresh-baked bread and battered cod fillets infused the air.

"Aww, fish and chips," Chase smiled. "My favorites."

"Fridays are always fish and Chips," Cassie grinned, filling a platter to overflowing with the crisp brown fillets. "Let's grab some beer and eat outside on the terrace."

Popping a tasty morsel into his mouth, he smiled, following Cassie outside with the beer.

"I hope you don't mind. I gave the staff the night off after dinner."

"Are you kidding? Babe, trust me, my world doesn't include staff. Knowing that we have this entire place to ourselves is unbelievable. Your mom was kind to invite me for the weekend."

"I think she likes you."

"Well, after having dinner with your parents, that's good to hear. Because I think we can both agree that your father doesn't share those sentiments."

Climbing into Chase's lap, Cassie lovingly put her arms around his neck as she softly ran her fingers through his dark military crew cut.

"Chase, as you've said, there's only two of us in this relationship. If you haven't noticed, I'm a grown woman, and I don't give a damn what my parents think, especially my father," Cassie giggled.

"Sweetheart, I think it's safe to say I've noticed," Chase whispered, pulling Cassie closer as he lovingly consumed her with a kiss. "Let's go inside."

Scooping her into his arms, he carried her inside and upstairs to the main suite. He knew every moment he shared with Cassie was a gift. Fueled with passion, they barely came up for air during the evening. As the early morning sun crept into their room, it found them awake, still wrapped in each other's arms. Basking in the warm afterglow of an unforgettable night, Cassie became emotional as a tear slowly escaped her moist eyes. Wiping her face, Chase sensed her worries.

Trying to hide her feelings, she prayed Chase wouldn't notice. She had to shove thoughts of his possible deployment to the farthest depths of her mind. She knew that she would never be ready to let him go.

This weekend was to create lasting memories, not be held hostage to her emotions.

"Sweetheart, why are you emotional?" Chase asked, softly wiping away her tears. "What's wrong? I hope you're not overthinking the deployment issue again."

"Chase, you can't leave. You just can't. I could never make it without you. I'm not that strong," Cassie cried, unleashing a torrent of emotions. "I've got a terrible feeling this might be our last weekend together. It's like a bad omen, and I can't shake it. I'm terrified," she sobbed desperately.

Shocked by her sudden outburst, Chase had never seen Cassie utterly distraught. He had to dispel her worries even if he shared her fears.

"Cassie, there's no way for you to know that." Pulling her even tighter against his chest, he rocked her safely in his arms. Trying to remain stoic, he knew that ultimately she was possibly right. However, no one had ever divulged that Mad Dog and a few of the guys had received orders to Vietnam. So how was it that she had such dire premonitions? For the first time in weeks, her actions were alarming. The chance that he might receive orders was high, and he was also uncertain about their future. Admittedly, it was a horrible nightmare, and he didn't believe in omens.

"Let's make the most of this weekend. Your mom graciously invited me, and I expect you to give me the royal tour. Are you okay with that?"

"Yes."

"Why don't you jump in the shower, and afterward, I'll cook breakfast."

"Why don't we both jump in the shower? I'm sure the kitchen staff has returned and prepared breakfast."

"Wow, even better."

Holding Cassie under the warm water as it cascaded over them was cathartic. He knew he had to lighten her mood and eliminate any further worries.

"So, what is there to do on this island of yours?" Chase teased, reaching for the shampoo.

"Well, for starters, I thought we could rent bikes. It's the best way to see the coast," Cassie smiled, gently lathering his chiseled abs.

"Now, that's my girl. Your smile has returned."

Reaching up on her toes, she lovingly caressed his face. Running her fingers through his day's growth of dark stubble, she knew her heart belonged to him. It was easy to envision their future together.

"Lieutenant Morgan, have I told you how much I love you?"

"Yes, but remind me?" Chase winked with a smile.

Stepping out of the shower and quickly getting dressed, they hurried downstairs to the kitchen.

After enjoying a simple breakfast of kippers, mushrooms, and eggs, James gave them a lift to a local bike rental. Deciding to rent individual bikes easily appeared to be the perfect way to explore the island. Nothing could be better than spending the entire day outdoors, with sunshine and the cool refreshing breezes wafting in from the ocean.

Taking a backward glance toward Chase, Cassie laughed. He looked totally out of his comfort zone. Wobbling along as his long legs straddled the short, rickety bike, it gave him a clown-like appearance.

"Okay, Flyboy, follow me."

After riding a short distance, she decided to give Chase's long legs a break. Stopping at the entrance to a narrow trail that led down to the shore, she knew it offered spectacular views. Leaving their bikes near the road, she eagerly took Chase's hand, pulling him near the cliff's edge. Overlooking the rocky terrain that descended steeply to the water's edge was intimidating.

"Aren't the views gorgeous?" Cassie stated. With windswept hair, she approached the narrow trail and, without hesitation, stepped over the first boulder as she began the formidable descent.

"Oh my God, Babe, this doesn't look safe," Chase gasped, taking his first step. Determined to keep his fears in check, he focused on the extraordinary vista as he followed close behind. The dark blue water glistened as it reflected the sun's early morning rays. Finally, reaching the shore, it seemed the risk was worth the heart-stopping moments to enjoy the beauty and seclusion.

"What do you think? Isn't it beautiful?"

"Yes. I'll have to admit it's spectacular, but the path getting here was a little intimidating."

"Geez, Chase, you fly jets, and you're afraid of heights."

"Sweetheart, it would have been easier to use a parachute than descend that trail."

"Well, we made it. Let's go swimming."

Before he could even question the fact that they had no swimsuits, Cassie began removing her clothes.

"Are you just going to stand there, or are you going to join me?" she taunted, quickly removing her jeans.

Watching as Cassie stripped down to her undergarments, Chase winked with a smile. "Oh, I'm fine. I'm just enjoying the view."

He finally removed his shirt with no one in sight, stripping down to his briefs. Then, following Cassie as she sprinted into the water, he forgot how bitterly cold the ocean was surrounding the British Isles.

Cassie screamed as an incoming wave immersed them in the frigid current. Rushing back to shore, Cassie shivered from the cold. Even the sun's warmth wasn't enough to stop the spread of goosebumps from overtaking her petite body. Immediately, Chase pulled her close to give her warmth. Even though he also felt the bitter sting of the numbing cold water, he quickly reached for his shirt. Wrapping her tight, he shielded her from the cool ocean breeze.

"Sorry," Cassie giggled. "That was freezing."

"Yes. It's definitely not the Mediterranean."

Keeping her close, Chase laughed. Then, gently, pulling her long wet curls away from her face, he kissed the nape of her neck. "I can't wait to see what other ideas you have."

"Oh, Lieutenant Morgan, are you doubting my abilities as a tour guide."

"I think I'll just keep that to myself," Chase whispered, pressing his lips to hers.

Cassie closed her eyes, melting into the warmth of his kiss. Loving Chase was as natural as breathing. Trying to purge her mind of the possibility this could be their last weekend together, she buried her face against his chest. Attempting to hide her tears, she had to keep her emotions in check.

"Okay, Sweetheart, what's next?" Chase teased.

"Let's get dressed. I think a stiff drink is in order. Then, I'll take you to my favorite pub. It's nearby."

"Great. I'll need a drink after I hike up this cliff."

Walking into the White Horse Pub, the locals were familiar with prominent families who lived on the island. Treated with respect, Cassie was free to be herself and not scrutinized by those who frequented the pub. Finding a table in the back, Chase ordered drinks, an orange shandy for Cassie, and his favorite, a New Castle Brown Ale.

"What do you suggest?" he asked, staring at the menu.

"I like bangers and mash. It's sausages with mashed potatoes. Why don't we start with that and order trifle for dessert? You'll love trifle. It's a layered sponge cake filled with fruit jams, egg custard, and topped with whipped cream."

"Okay. I'm not hungry, but if those are your favorites, I can't wait to try them."

"Well, we could make it just one order and share," Cassie offered.

"Sounds like a plan," Chase winked, tossing back a huge gulp of New Castle Brown Ale.

Pensively staring into her gorgeous blue eyes, he reached over gently taking Cassie's hand. He wanted to know more about the countess. This brave woman chose to verbally stand against her husband at dinner and graciously offered him the opportunity to visit the Isle of Wight. "Sweetheart, today has been incredible, thanks to your mom. How is she doing healthwise? I know you said she has kidney disease and is undergoing dialysis. I appreciate the fact she let me come down with you."

"Chase, that's thoughtful of you to ask about my mom. She has good days and bad days. My father has a private nurse for her and a room set up to undergo dialysis at home safely. To be honest, I'm extremely concerned about her. She hasn't been feeling well. I know she worries about me, and I think it's one of the reasons she knew that I could use a getaway. Caring for a loved one is difficult."

"Cassie, if you ever need me, please call at any time, day or night. You have the house number in Mildenhall."

"Thanks." Giving him a quick kiss as the waiter sat a piping hot plate on the table, Cassie smiled. "Try this," she offered, serving him a bite of sausage covered in mashed potatoes with onion gravy.

"Oh my gosh, that's ridiculously good."

"Told you." Tasting a large bite, Cassie moaned. "Scrumptious."

Cutting a larger piece, Cassie again smothered the sausage in potatoes and gravy, lifting the fork to his mouth. "I think you enjoy feeding me," Chase laughed, consuming the bite. Then, ordering another round of drinks, the waiter brought out dessert.

"Okay, try it," Cassie laughed, spooning a large portion of the trifle for him to taste.

"Wow, that's amazing," Chase grinned, wiping his mouth. "Another, please, don't stop." Taking a larger piece of sponge cake onto the spoon with jam and custard, Cassie once again lifted it to his mouth. Being silly, he licked his lips as he devoured the tasty British dessert.

"Now, it's my turn," Chase smiled, lifting a large spoonful to Cassie's mouth. "Yummy. I think we're going to need two spoons," she laughed.

Sitting next to the love of his life, he thought it was perhaps the best meal he had ever eaten. But, he knew that even though the food was incredible, it had more to do with the beautiful young woman sitting next to him. Thoughts of moving their relationship to the next level entered his mind. Cassie was everything he had ever wanted in life.

"Okay, Lady Cromwell, what's next on your agenda?"

"Well, Lieutenant Morgan, why don't we ride back to the manor house. After consuming all this rich food, how does a game of tennis sound? We can work off all these calories. Tomorrow we can tour Queen Victoria's home and gardens."

"Sounds great. However, I must warn you. I'm a pro at tennis."

"Oh yeah, we'll see about that. I'll race you back."

"You're on. Lead the way."

Riding back to the estate, Cassie left him behind to deal with his wobbly bike when they left the pub. His bike continued to sway as he once again tried to regain control. However, not one to give up easily, he was determined to give it his all despite the fact his long legs were still at odds with the short, clumsy bike. Cassie laughed. "Come on, lieutenant. You can do better than that."

"Not on this decrepit contraption," Chase complained.

"I'll have to admit. It definitely wasn't the right fit for you and your long legs. Let's walk. It isn't much further."

Pushing their bikes along the road's edge, Cassie smiled at his tenacity. She knew he wasn't the type to give up easily, and she knew these were traits she was looking for in a partner.

Staring at Cassie, she was gorgeous, fun, and carefree as the wind tousled her golden curls. Chase knew their chance meeting in London had brought him more happiness than any man deserved.

Returning the bikes, they received a full refund on his ill-fitted bicycle. Then, deciding to walk the short distance back to the estate was less than a thirty-minute hike. Once again, they entered the kitchen in search of a cold beverage.

"That was fun," Cassie laughed, handing him a chilled beer from the fridge as she quickly downed a bottle of water.

Tossing back the entire beer in a few gulps, Chase grinned, wiping his mouth.

"No more bicycles, only Vespas," he teased.

"Agreed. You looked pretty ridiculous, trying to keep yourself from falling off. Are you sure you fly jets?"

"Oh, Sweetheart, I wouldn't go there if I were you," Chase winked with a naughty smile.

"Well, let's see how good you are at tennis."

"It's on. Let's go."

Hurriedly, changing clothes and shoes, they walked across the massive manicured lawns to the tennis court. After playing several sets, Chase had been true to his word. He easily won each match, making it look all too easy.

"Okay. Maybe we've discovered something that you're good at," Cassie teased, wiping the sweat from her forehead. "Let's go inside. I think we could use a shower before dinner."

"I like the sound of that," Chase grinned, putting his arm around Cassie as they slowly made their way back to the main house.

A delectable aroma of braised beef with all the trimmings infused the air as they entered the stately home.

"I hope you're hungry. I gave specific instructions regarding the menu options during our stay."

"It smells phenomenal, but I have other things on my mind at the moment, which don't include food," Chase whispered.

"Lieutenant Morgan, you're a bad boy?"

"Lady Cromwell," he paused. "Are you implying that you don't like bad boys? Surely, you jest," he winked wickedly.

"Well, Flyboy, you might be the exception," she blushed.

Like rambunctious teenagers, they raced upstairs to the main suite. Clothes began hitting the floor as soon as the door opened. Then, playfully pulling Cassie into the shower, it suddenly became steamy and not necessarily due to the hot water trickling over them. "Chase, I love you," Cassie whispered.

"Cassie, I've loved you since our eyes first met. I couldn't imagine my life without you," Chase responded, softly kissing the nape of her neck.

His feelings for Cassie felt right in every way, and taking their commitment to the next level seemed only a natural progression. It was a pivotal turning point, and he was finally confident she shared his feelings. There was no longer any doubt that he would propose to the beautiful girl in his arms. Regardless of the fact she was nobility, her father's dislike for him, or the possibility he could be deployed, nothing would stop him. He was determined to get down on one knee and ask the most critical question of his life. He just needed to arrange the logistics and shop for an engagement ring.

Stepping out of the shower before they withered away, Chase grabbed towels to wrap around Cassie and himself. Unexpectedly, Cassie's eyes moistened as a tear escaped, slowly making its way down her face. Hoping he wouldn't notice. Once again, she had allowed thoughts of his possible deployment to creep into her mind. Overwhelmed with emotions, she hoped he wouldn't detect her worries. However, he always sensed her feelings.

"Babe, are you alright?" Chase worried.

"I'm fine. Trust me. It's nothing."

"Well, it doesn't seem like nothing. What's wrong?"

Perhaps, Cassie needed the confidence a ring on her left hand could provide. However, having second thoughts, Chase knew she deserved a proposal that took a little time and effort. The fact that he didn't even have an engagement ring made his decision to wait easy. Once he arrived back in Mildenhall, he would find the perfect engagement ring and plan an unforgettable proposal. A huge smile slowly crept over his face at the mere prospect. His girl deserved the very best.

"I'm starved. Do you think dinner is ready?" Chase questioned, trying to lighten the mood.

"I'm sure, but if I didn't know you better, I would certainly think there's something you're not telling me," Cassie smirked. "You seemed distracted."

"Sweetheart, how could you possibly think anything is wrong. Just look at this place. It's incredible. Being here alone with you would be any man's dream. Now, let's get dressed and enjoy dinner."

The dining room was glowing with the soft ambiance of lit candles. The massive oak table appeared eloquently set as if it awaited the arrival of a king and queen.

"Wow. I feel underdressed," Chase smiled, looking down at his jeans and t-shirt.

"Don't be silly," Cassie laughed, taking his hand as she led him to a seat next to her. "I love you in jeans and a T-shirt. It reflects your muscular abs and that you live at the gym.

Staring at the intricate tableware, he again felt like a fish out of water. He wasn't one to be impressed by wealth or possessions. However, he was smart enough to know that he had the best thing in the world sitting next to him, and soon they would share all their tomorrows.

"Let's take our wine and go outside," Cassie suggested, finishing the last bite of her Tiramisu.

"Whatever my lady wants," Chase laughed, pulling back Cassie's chair.

"Chase, that's not funny. There are no titles when we're together. I don't give a damn about titles or nobility. Titles don't make my father a better man."

"Point duly noted," Chase winked with a smile.

Sitting outside on the terrace beneath a dark purple sky filled with a plethora of twinkling stars, Cassie cuddled inside the warmth of his arms. If there were moments of perfection in one's life, this would top his list.

Later that night, Cassie playfully pulled the covers over their heads. Passion simply consumed every second of their night. Once again, they were awake to welcome the early rays of the morning sun. Cassie not only warmed his bed, she also warmed his heart.

The following day found them exploring the Osborne House, the country home of Queen Victoria, and enjoying a picnic lunch near the Needles Lighthouse. Their weekend on the Isle of Wight was coming to an end. It had been the catalyst that Chase needed to make life-changing decisions.

Boarding their flight back to Mildenhall early Sunday morning, Chase was a man on a mission. Thoughts of finding the perfect ring and setting up the perfect proposal venue filled his mind. First, of course, he would need a best man, and he had the ideal candidate waiting for his arrival.

Chapter Nine

"Oh my, look what the cat dragged in. Welcome home," Chris laughed. "Sit down, Buddy, and give me all the details."

"Geez. Who are you? My therapist?"

"If you need a therapist. I'm happy to help. Just have a seat on my couch. I'll grab us a cold New Castle."

"Chris, I could use a confidant. But, I swear if any of this gets out at work, I'm coming for you, and I promise it won't be pretty.

"Buddy, trust me, my face couldn't take another assault. I'd probably be scarred for life, and I'm afraid you might not fare as well either," Chris countered, tossing a bottle of ale to his client.

"Well," Chase paused, taking a slow sip of the cold brew. "I've decided that I'm going to propose to Cassie." Then, lounging back on the sofa, he waited pensively for Chris's reaction.

"Oh my God," Chris gasped, choking on the ale as it spewed from his mouth and nostrils. "Holy hell." Coughing uncontrollably, he recovered his breath.

"Damn, hang on, Buddy. I'll get you a paper towel. Unfortunately, your etiquette skills are lacking. "Here. Clean yourself up," Chase smirked, running back from the kitchen. Chris's reaction was comical.

"Sorry, but, as your therapist, hell, I take that back, as your friend,

I think you know what I'm going to say. Are you out of your frigging mind? You can't marry that girl. Seriously, Chase, you must be crazy."

"Listen, Chris, our little session is over. I'm not asking your permission to live my life. I love Cassie, and after this weekend, I have no doubts the feeling is mutual."

"Chase, does the fact that her real name is Lady Cassandra Cromwell mean anything to you or that her dad hates Americans?"

"No."

"I guess that says it all," Chris retorted. "Now, I'm certain that you've lost your frigging mind. Look, Buddy, Uncle Sam pays you to fly F-4s, not get besotted with someone. Granted, I'll agree Cassie is gorgeous. She's a great girl, and she'll make someone a wonderful wife one day. But Chase, that someone isn't you. I don't mean to burst your bubble," Chris explained, downing a huge gulp of ale. "Buddy, she's way out of your league."

"Chris, I hear your concerns, and I understand your comments. However, none of it matters. I don't expect you to understand. I genuinely don't. To be honest, I knew exactly how you would react. However, none of it changes anything. I love her, and I'm going to propose. End of the discussion."

"Buddy, if there's been any truth spoken here, one thing rings true. It is your life, and if you want to screw it up, who am I to stand in your way."

"Does that mean you'll be my best man?"

"Oh, hell, I suppose. I need another New Castle. Want one?"

"Yeah, but there's something else," Chase smirked. "Stay put. I'll get the New Castles."

"Damn, man, don't tell me you knocked her up?"

"Seriously, Chris, that's hilarious," Chase laughed, retrieving more ale from the kitchen.

Handing Chris a bottle of the cold brew, Chase once again lounged back on the sofa. "Do you believe in premonitions?"

"No."

"Well, you might after hearing what happened," he grimaced, tossing back a sip of ale. "Cassie had a premonition or omen. I think she referred to it as an omen. To make a long story short, Cassie thinks I'm going to get orders to Vietnam. And, trust me when I say this, she was more than upset. She was devastated."

"Damn. You do know Cassie could be right. We both know it's only a matter of time. Did you tell her that Mad Dog got orders?"

"Oh, hell, no. I would never have told Cassie, and there's no way that she knows about Mad Dog. But I'll have to admit it is a little disturbing. More than anything, it's the timing. Her mother is in failing health, and her dad isn't supportive. They don't have a great relationship. I'm not sure Cassie is strong enough to make it on her own if I get deployed," Chase frowned, reaching for another New Castle.

"Geez, Chase, that is worrisome, but I'm sure Cassie is stronger than you think, and it was only a suspicion. I wouldn't lose any sleep over it."

"Yeah. I guess you're right. Speaking of sleep, I think I'm going to turn in for the night. Oh, before I forget, did you see Darcy this weekend?"

"Yep. We'll save that discussion for tomorrow. It's good to have you back."

"Thanks."

"By the way, I hear therapists are expensive. So you'll get my bill?"

"Right. Don't hold your breath on that one," Chase laughed, running upstairs. "Goodnight."

"See you in the morning. No worries, Buddy," Chris responded.

The next day found Chase and Chris ready to start another work week. Driving into the base, Chase inquired about Chris's weekend.

"So, how was your weekend? You mentioned last night that you met up with Darcy," Chase questioned, taking a sip of coffee as he turned onto the narrow single-track road leading into the base.

"Yes. It was great. Darcy invited me out to the beach house. Man, that place is spectacular and right on the water."

"Did you stay overnight?" Chase smirked.

"No. It wasn't that kind of evening. Darcy and I are just friends. She made pizza, and we roasted marshmallows. She's fun to be with, and it sure beats staying at home watching British game shows."

"I'm happy that you both had a great Saturday."

"Thanks."

Walking into the squadron for their morning training briefing, the worries of Cassie's premonition still haunted him. However, there was no mention of anyone receiving orders. With Mad Dog no longer occupying the second seat as his weapons systems officer, Wizzo, things appeared subdued as he walked out to the flight line.

Climbing into the cockpit of the F-4 Phantom, Chase loved flying. It was his reason for joining the Air Force and attending the academy. Lieutenant Wagner, who had just arrived from the states, was now filling the position vacated by Mad Dog.

"All set, Lieutenant Wagner?" Chase questioned as the canopy closed. Then, removing the chocks from under the tires, the crew chief signaled him toward the runway. Getting airborne and accomplishing the training mission erased any further worries about deployment.

Later that afternoon, after deciding not to stop at the Officer's Club but rather at the Class Six Store and the Commissary, they were finally ready to leave the base and call it a day. Chase was anxious to get home and call Darcy. He wanted her input regarding the best jewelry stores' location, which meant he would have to trust her with his plans. The beach house in Hunstanton also topped his list of places to propose. It was private, and a walk along the beach at sunset seemed perfect.

Arriving back at the tiny row house and hurriedly putting away their week's supply of groceries, Chase raced upstairs to make the call. Darcy answered on the first ring.

"Hello."

"Darcy, do you have a few minutes?"

"Lieutenant Morgan," Darcy giggled. "I heard your weekend was nearly perfect, except for your bike rental. Although, I'll have to admit Cassie made it sound hilarious."

"Well, that's not why I called."

"So, what's up?"

"I think you should sit down."

"I am sitting. You're scaring me."

"Sorry, it's nothing ominous. Trust me." Chase sat down on his bed, worried if her reaction was like Chris's that perhaps they should have had this discussion in person.

"First, you don't have a drink in your hand, do you?" he laughed.

"No. You're silly. What's going on?"

"Well," Chase paused. "I'm going to propose to Cassie."

"What? What did you say? I'm not sure I heard you."

"Now, you're the one being silly. I said that I'm going to propose to Cassie," Chase reiterated.

"Oh, my god. Does she know?"

"No."

"Chase, as I told you once before, you're crazier than a bag full of ferrets."

"Listen, Darcy. I'm serious."

"Listen, Chase. You're crazy."

"I need your help."

"I'm not sure I want to be involved," Darcy vented. "You do remember that I said her dad hates Yanks, and have you forgotten her title. Damn, Chase, I like you, and you're a great friend, but I'm sorry, Cassie is way out of your league."

"Hell, Darcy, now you're acting like Chris."

"Has it crossed your mind that Chris and I possibly gave you good advice? Of course, Chase, you might not like our opinions, but if you're a smart guy, you'll rethink this craziness."

"Darcy, I hear what you're saying, but I will tell you what I told Chris."

"Oh yeah, and what would that be?"

"I'm not asking your permission to live my life. I love Cassie, and after this past weekend, I have no doubt that she feels the same. I'm proposing. So, I guess you have to decide if you will help."

"What did Chris say?"

"Let's just say he agreed to be my best man."

"Oh, hell, Chase, what do you need me to do? However, so that you know, I still think this is crazy. I hope you don't crash and burn," Darcy laughed.

"Thanks, Darcy, for your assuring vote of confidence. First, I thought you might suggest a great jewelry store, and second, I wondered if I could use the beach house."

"Yes. I'm completely barmy for agreeing to this, but I also enjoy a great love story, and this is one for the books. I have no doubts that Cassie is head over heels in love with you. You're a lucky guy," Darcy cried.

"Damn, are you crying?"

"My best friend is about to get engaged. I think I'm entitled."

"Geez, between Chris choking on his ale and your crying, I think I'm the only sane one."

"Whatever. I'll go with you to London this weekend. Our family has a fabulous jeweler, and I'm sure you'll find the perfect ring. Oh, and bring your best man. I'll see you Saturday."

"Thanks, Darcy."

Hanging up the phone, Chase laid back on the bed. Finally, his plan was coming together. He had the picture-perfect place to propose, and after this weekend, he would have the perfect ring.

Running downstairs to get a beer, Chris was in the kitchen making tacos.

"So, how did that go? Your conversation with Darcy?"

"Let's just say we're going to London this weekend to purchase a ring. By the way, Darcy wants your crazy ass to come along."

"Really," Chris smiled.

"Don't make any plans for Saturday. Guess we'll have to skip our date at the gym."

"Breaks my heart. Have a taco."

After a long week at work and more time in the air than even Chase liked, the weekend finally arrived. Telling his first white lie to Cassie, she assumed he was on alert duty.

Hearing a light knock, Chris raced over to the door.

"Well, this is a first. I'm taking two handsome pilots to London. Are you guys ready?"

"Yes," Chris smiled, yelling for Chase. "You look nice," he added.

"Thanks. I'm driving. Hope you flight jockeys can deal with it," Darcy snickered.

"That remains to be seen," Chase laughed, bounding down the stairs. "Back seat," he demanded, glancing at Chris.

"Really. You know I fly front seat."

"Not today, buddy."

Getting into the back seat of Darcy's new black BMW, Chris worried for their safety.

"I hope we don't need barf bags," he roared.

"Seriously. I'm a great driver," Darcy laughed, revving the engine as she entered the motorway heading south toward London. "It's only about an hour and a half."

Later arriving at the jewelry store, Darcy assured Chase that he would get a great deal. Walking inside, she had scheduled an appointment. Taking a glance at the numerous sparkling display cases, Chase was entirely overwhelmed. Case after case of glimmering diamonds awaited his perusal. Not knowing where to start, the owner presented him with a few options. Finally, after what seemed like an eternity, Chase's eye caught the sparkles of a two-carat heart-shaped ring. It wasn't ostentatious. However, on closer inspection, it was perfect. It reflected a kaleidoscope of brilliant colors. Deciding to purchase the matching wedding bands, he was confident with his choices. After Darcy and the owner had a private discussion, the price was lowered and finally affordable. Even though it would make a sizeable dent in his savings account, he knew the damage would have been worse without Darcy's help. As the owner handed him the tiny velvet box, he was another step closer to getting down on one knee.

Leaving the shop, Darcy had a great idea. "Are you guys hungry?"

"Are you kidding? I'm starving," Chris answered.

"Lunch is on me. Why don't we go to the Boar's Head? It's just around the corner and where you met Cassie."

"Oh, my God, you are romantic," Chase laughed.

"That works for me," Chris smiled, getting in the back seat.

Arriving at the pub, they found a quiet booth in the back. Picking up the menu, Chase already knew what he wanted. He was ordering bangers and mash. Watching as Darcy and Chris began tossing back one too many beers, Chase slowly nursed his one drink. He knew that someone had to step up and become the responsible designated driver.

Even though he didn't consider himself overly romantic, visions of the day he met Cassie flooded his mind. It was hard sitting in the Boar's Head without her. Looking toward the pub entrance, he visualized the evening she walked in. Whether it was karma or destiny, they were fated to meet. Taking the tiny box out of his pocket, he gazed at the shimmering diamond. It was hard to comprehend that they had met in this pub only a few months ago. Now he was one step closer to making their relationship permanent. Noticing his intense stare at the ring, Darcy worried he might be rethinking his selection. However, she knew that Cassie would love it.

"I hope you're not doubting your decision. It's gorgeous, and Cassie will love it."

"No. I'm just a little sentimental. It's hard to sit here and not think of the gorgeous girl who will hopefully wear it. The Boar's Head will always be that one place that she and I will continue to revisit. How can we not? We met here."

"Chase, I was here. Remember? Trust me. She's bonkers over you. If I know one thing, you're the only guy for her. Cassie has never had a lot of boyfriends, and she tells me everything?"

"Everything?" Chase questioned.

Darcy grinned. "Everything."

"Geez, that's a bit intimidating," he smirked, choking on his ale. Then, wiping the foamy brew from his mouth, he blushed.

"Well, lieutenant, now, you know."

Tossing her car keys toward him, Darcy realized her limits.

"Do you mind? I think Chris and I have had too much to drink."

"No worries. Watching as you both drank like a fish, I knew someone had to be the responsible adult. So I'll drive us."

"If you can fly jets, I think you're capable of driving my BMW and managing the motorways," Darcy giggled, finishing her shandy.

Chris laughed, downing his pint of Guinness. "Oh, I'm not so sure. Chase has had a few close calls passing lorries."

"Thanks, buddy, for your vote of confidence. Maybe you would rather walk," Chase vented.

Leaving the Boar's Head, Chase was in a somber mood. Even though eating at the pub was near the jewelry store and a great idea, it made him keenly aware that he was missing Cassie. Arriving back at Mildenhall, Darcy agreed to contact Cassie and have her call him.

Finally, hearing the phone ring, Chase bolted up the stairs.

"Hello."

"Chase, I thought you were on duty at the alert pad today?" Cassie questioned.

"I got off early." His response was just a varied continuation of the first white lie. No one ever got off early. "How was your day?"

"Boring. I missed you."

"Sweetheart, I missed you too. Do you think you could get away tomorrow?"

"I'll try."

"Why don't you come over. I'll cook dinner."

"Okay. What time?"

"Seriously, Babe, as soon as you get up in the morning. I don't care. Now would work. Why don't you come over now? You could stay the night?"

"Really. Chase, you sound desperate?" Cassie giggled.

"Okay, so I'm desperate. What's your point? You don't miss me?"

"Flyboy, of course, I miss you. Desperately, I might add. You're silly."

"I'll call Darcy and ask her to bring you over. Tonight."

"Alright. You better at least have pizza."

"Great. See you soon. Love you, Babe."

"Love you too."

Calling Darcy, Chase had to ensure that Cassie wouldn't need George, and he was sure Darcy also loved pizza.

"Hello."

"Darcy, I need a favor."

"Chase, when do you not need a favor. What's up?"

"I need you to bring Cassie over tonight. I'll get a pizza."

"Geez, Chase, we just got back from London."

"Sorry. I know Cassie doesn't drive, and I don't want George to bring her. It might not go well if her dad found out."

"Okay. I'll bring Cassie over later tonight. No worries. See you soon."

"Thanks."

Running downstairs, he needed to inform Chris of his plans. He was instantly on board and offered to make homemade pizzas. A delicious aroma of baked breadsticks and pizza soon infused their tiny house. Covered in flour from head to toe after helping Chris in the kitchen, Chase went upstairs to shower and change clothes before the girls arrived. The night was off to a great start.

Hearing a knock at the door, Chris wiped his hands and walked out to answer the door, forgetting that he was covered in flour.

"Hey, come in. You're early."

"Oh my gosh, you look like an explosion in a bakery. What happened?" Darcy laughed.

"Oh, that," Chris grinned, wiping flour off his clothes. "I decided to make pizzas, and Chase offered to help. We were goofing around, and the next thing I knew, Chase was throwing flour. He wouldn't stop, and my spotless kitchen was covered in flour, so I had to retaliate."

"Geez, you're both acting like two crazy toddlers. I'll help you clean up the kitchen. I can only imagine the mess you guys made. Let's go," Darcy snickered, leading Chris into the kitchen.

"Where's Chase?" Cassie laughed.

"Oh, he's upstairs taking a shower."

Running upstairs, Cassie smiled at the thought of finding Chase covered in flour. Then, hearing the water in the shower, she walked into the bathroom.

Surprising Chase, Cassie laughed as she suddenly threw back the shower curtain. "Heard there was an explosion of flour in the kitchen."

"Cassie," Chase grinned wickedly, grabbing her as he pulled her into the shower fully clothed. "I hope you brought a change of clothes."

He quickly pulled her into his arms, making love like two star-crossed lovers given a reprieve to spend eternity together. His love for Cassie knew no bounds.

Touching his face, she felt like the luckiest girl on earth. "I love you, Flyboy."

"I know," he whispered, playfully kissing the nape of her neck. "I know."

The following evening as Cassie left, he knew without a doubt that he was ready to take their relationship to the next level.

Chapter Ten

The following week went by in a blur as Chase put together all the final touches for his proposal. Darcy stocked the beach house at Hunstanton with everything they might need. She even arranged catering to have Cassie's favorite meal waiting for when they arrived. Florists were on standby to inundate the house's entire bottom level with bouquets of pink roses and peonies while Chase proposed on the beach. If everything went according to plan, they would return to discover lit candles, fresh flowers, and a chilled magnum of Moet & Chandon. Chase prayed for a day filled with sunshine and a gorgeous sunset. However, the only thing which genuinely mattered was hearing the love of his life say *yes* to spending all their tomorrows together.

Arriving home late Friday evening, the phone was ringing. Chase hurriedly unlocked the door, trying desperately to catch the call. Thankfully, Darcy left a message to inform him that she would stop by and drop off the keys to the beach house.

Later that night, sleep didn't come easy. Chase's mind was on overload. He tossed and turned, filled with thoughts of everything that could go wrong and praying for everything to go right. Glancing at the clock, it was early, 5:00 a.m. Getting up was his only recourse. Staying in bed offered him no chance of rest. However, a hot cup of coffee seemed a great alternative. Grabbing his bathrobe, he went downstairs.

Plugging in the electric kettle, Chase reached into the cabinet for a tall mug. Walking over to the kitchen window, he drew back the curtains. Instantly, the bright rays of the morning sun flooded the tiny space. Finally, it appeared the weather might cooperate with his plans with a bit of luck. Pouring a cup of the hot brew, he sat down at the kitchen table. Thoughts of Cassie and the day ahead overwhelmed him. In just a few short hours, he would be on his way to the beach house with the love of his life. Hearing footsteps descending the stairs, the robust aroma of coffee had awakened Chris.

"Geez, Buddy, did you get any sleep?" Chris reacted, reaching for a cup.

"No."

"I figured as much. The smell of coffee woke me, and I thought you might need someone to talk to."

Pouring himself a cup, Chris sat down at the table across from him, noting his confused stare as he sipped his hot beverage.

"Chase, I love you like a brother, and Cassie is one lucky girl. Hell, you're a lucky guy. I know I might have questioned your sanity, but I want you to know that as your best friend, I support your decision, and I wish you the best."

"Thanks."

"Do you need help with anything? I'm going to catch a ride to the base with Stevenson and work out at the gym."

"No. Darcy is going to drop Cassie off around noon. She's taken care of all the arrangements."

"Alright, buddy, I'm going to take a shower. Talk to you later. Good luck."

"Thanks. Oh, don't use all the hot water," Chase laughed.

Later that morning, hearing a faint knock at the door, he knew the girls had arrived. It was the beginning of a day that hopefully would change his entire future.

Cassie had no idea of the extensive plans or the impending proposal as they drove out to Hunstanton Beach. Their conversation was light and easy-going, with no hint of what was soon to unfold.

Arriving at the sprawling beach house, sounds resonating from a warm crackling fire and soft music welcomed them. The ambiance was romantic as floor-to-ceiling windows immersed the expansive living room in a soft glow. Taking Cassie's hand, Chase pulled her towards the back of the room. The wall of windows revealed a breathtaking view of the sparkling blue hues of the ocean. The aroma of simmering roast beef and trimmings infused the air. As was usual for Darcy, she always had the kitchen staff prepare meals. However, today she gave specific instructions to prepare Cassie's favorite foods and set the atmosphere for her arrival.

"Wow, something smells heavenly," Cassie smiled. Then, removing her shoes, she ran into the kitchen. She smiled, discovering roast beef with root vegetables, warm bread, and a large trifle sitting on the island. "Is there something I missed? Are we celebrating?"

"Yes. The fact that we have another weekend all to ourselves. Darcy even had the kitchen staff prepare your favorite meal. I hope you approve."

"Are you kidding? I'm starved. I skipped breakfast this morning." Lifting the cover from the roasting pan, Cassie ravenously devoured a carrot.

Opening a bottle of wine, Chase reached for glasses as Cassie found plates and cutlery. Deciding to eat inside where it was warm rather than dining on the patio with the cool ocean breeze, the weekend was off to a great start. Cassie went back for seconds, making the idea of her favorite meal a huge success.

"I suppose I owe Darcy a return favor. It was scrumptious," Cassie mentioned, wiping her mouth as she finished the last morsel on her plate.

"Definitely," Chase agreed, refilling their wine glasses. "Why don't we take our drinks to the other room and sit by the fire?"

"Sounds good." Feeling a little tipsy, Chase wrapped his arms around Cassie as they made their way to the living room.

Tossing some large decorative pillows onto the floor in front of the fireplace, Chase pulled Cassie down next to him. "Sweetheart, you have no idea how much I've looked forward to this weekend," Chase winked, pulling the love of his life into his arms as they snuggled. "Did you have any problems getting away for the weekend?"

"No. My mother is aware that we are spending the weekend together, but we chose not to tell my father. My life simply works better that way, at least, for the present. So we have the entire weekend to ourselves." Staring into the depths of Chase's blue eyes, Cassie cherished every moment they had together despite her father's disapproval.

Chase regretted that he couldn't properly ask for Cassie's hand in marriage, as the custom would have been. But, knowing her father's disdain for Americans had left him with no recourse than to proceed without her father's approval. Having a lengthy discussion with Jaclyn, Cassie's mother, she assured him that her husband wouldn't stand in the way of their daughter's happiness. But unfortunately, time might not be on their side, and waiting wasn't an option.

"Let's check out the BBC. I think Casablanca is on this afternoon. I love old movies," Cassie suggested.

"Okay, if that's what you want to do," Chase smirked, looking down at his watch. It barely left enough time to indulge in a movie before the florists and catering were due to arrive in less than two hours.

"We need popcorn. I'll be right back," Cassie suggested, pulling away from the warmth of his arms as she made her way to the kitchen.

Hurriedly returning with popcorn and another bottle of wine, a rerun of the old classic was just airing. Taking a knitted afghan from the sofa, Cassie wrapped it around them, snuggling into Chase's arms as the movie began. Thankfully, Cassie was unaware that his focus wasn't entirely on watching Casablanca. Unknowingly, his concentration was elsewhere. It centered around a walk on the beach, him down on one knee, and praying Cassie said *yes*. Discreetly searching his pocket for the ring, he smiled, knowing the tiny box was secure.

As the movie ended, Chase's nerves became apparent as he fidgeted with the afghan. Then, trying to keep his anxieties under wrap, he reached for the opened bottle of wine.

"Let's have another glass of wine and stroll along the beach afterward.

We've been indoors all afternoon, and I think we could use some fresh air."

"Sounds good. You did sit through Casablanca," Cassie laughed, sipping wine. "Why don't we call Darcy and Chris and invite them over. There's a lot of food in the kitchen. We could have a marathon game night."

Hearing her suggestion, Chase smiled, knowing her idea would never materialize. If things went according to plan, having anyone join them would be utterly ridiculous.

"We'll see," he grinned seductively. "Maybe I want you all to myself."

"Wow, Flyboy, that sounds romantic," Cassie smiled, reaching over to give him a quick kiss, which effortlessly became heated and passionate. Reluctantly pulling away, he knew if things escalated at this moment, his entire plan would be in jeopardy.

"I think you agreed to join me for a walk. Are you ready?"

"Yes. First, I need something warmer to wear."

Waiting by the door, Cassie returned, looking radiant wearing denim jeans and a matching jacket. "I'm ready."

He reached for her hand and led Cassie outside and down the weathered walkway toward the beach. Suddenly a brisk wind blew through her long natural curls covering her eyes. Pausing to pull the blonde strands away from her face, he lovingly kissed the nape of her neck.

"You look beautiful."

"Awe, thanks, Flyboy," Cassie whispered.

Removing her shoes, she playfully teased the waves washing ashore with her toes. Then, strolling further down the beach, she leaned against Chase, savoring the magic of the evening.

Do you ever wish we could live like this forever?" Chase questioned, pulling her closer.

"Yes, silly, you know that I do."

Gazing upward into the starlit heavens, Chase stopped, praying this was his cue. Turning to face Cassie, he smiled. Momentarily mesmerized by the depths of her gorgeous blue eyes, Chase got down on one knee. Staring into her face, he smiled.

"Cassie, I love you. I want to spend all my tomorrows with you. I want to wake up with you in my arms every morning. I've loved you from the evening you walked into the pub. Marry me," Chase winked with a smile. Then, with his heart pounding like it was about to explode, he reached into his pocket for the exquisite ring.

"Oh my God," Cassie screamed. "Yes, yes, yes! I was beginning to think you would never ask." Stunned and ecstatic by the sudden proposal, she stared at the brilliant diamond as tears of joy flowed down her cheeks.

Chase knew their lives would never be the same as he placed the ring on her left hand. "I love you."

With tears flooding her face, Cassie jumped into Chase's arms. "I love you too, Flyboy."

Wrapped in Chase's arms, under an umbrella of shimmering stars, time stopped. Cassie loved him with every ounce of her being. Lost in his kiss, she knew she had everything she ever wanted. She had loved him from the moment they met.

"Cassie, I might not have a title before my name, but I promise to love you forever. I can't imagine my life without you."

"Chase, stop. Our relationship has never been about titles or nobility. I love you, Lieutenant Morgan, and I never want to live without you."

Chase knew his love for her was infinite, kissing away the tears that continued to cascade down Cassie's face. Together they could face any challenge.

"Let's walk back," he grinned mischievously.

"Yes," Cassie beamed, staring at her left hand.

Arriving back at the beach house, Chase opened the door.

Screams of delight filled the air as Cassie stood motionless, taking in the elaborate scene of pink flowers and lit candles.

"Oh my God, Chase, it's gorgeous," Cassie cried, entirely overwhelmed by the enormous display. "I love peonies and roses. How did you know, and how did you do this?"

"Well," Chase paused. "I had a little help."

"Darcy?"

"Yes. Darcy helped put it together, but it was entirely my idea."

"Chase, you're romantic. I love it."

Walking over to inhale the fragrant aroma of the fresh flowers, she wiped tears from her eyes.

"Thank you," she beamed, still reeling from the excitement. "I've never seen the beach house look so magnificent." Then, reaching up to kiss Chase, she felt like the luckiest girl on earth.

Opening the champagne, he filled two fluted glasses with the sparkling beverage. "I think this calls for a toast," Chase winked, handing Cassie a glass.

"To the future, Mrs. Morgan, you've made me the happiest guy in the world. You make my life complete."

"Chase, becoming Mrs. Morgan, rivals any royal title I could ever have. From the first time I saw you, it was love at first sight."

"Well, let's just hope we can convince your father."

"Stop. Please don't mention my father. There's no place for him here."

Sealing the toast with a kiss, Chase had other things on his mind, which didn't include discussing her father. Scooping Cassie into his arms, he followed a trail of pink rose petals leading upstairs to the main suite.

"Sweetheart, thank you for saying *yes*. Now, let me thank you properly," Chase whispered, laying Cassie on the bed covered in rose petals. Tonight was about making memories that would last a lifetime.

"You left the champagne downstairs," Cassie giggled.

"Really. You want more?" Chase questioned with a laugh.

Playfully pulling Chase down next to her, she smiled. "I'm joking, lieutenant. I have everything I need right here." Bringing his lips to meet hers. She was entirely lost in their kiss. Staring at her sexy fiance, the remaining hours of the evening passed in unrestrained passion.

Waking the following morning, Cassie lovingly caressed Chase's dark stubble, kissing him awake.

"Goodmorning, Lieutenant Morgan. Last night was unbelievable."

"Incredible," Chase grinned, slowly opening his eyes. Then, taking Cassie's left hand," he paused. "Awe, someone made out like a bandit."

"I love it. It's perfect," Cassie gleamed, admiring her new accessory.

After spending the morning leisurely in bed and later making pancakes, Chase was relieved. The weekend far exceeded anything he could've imagined. As they locked the door and walked away the following afternoon, the memories created inside would last a lifetime. There was no longer a doubt they would share all their tomorrows.

Chapter Eleven

Darcy and Chris planned a surprise celebration for Chase and Cassie the following weekend. The row house appeared the perfect place to keep the festivities private and away from the media. Choosing to cook rather than have the evening catered, Chris decided to prepare lasagna. Leaving work early on Friday evening, he caught a ride home. Arriving before Chase and Cassie, it left just enough time to decorate the tiny flat and get the meal prep well underway.

Hearing a light knock, Chris walked over to open the door. Darcy looked comical, trying to balance shopping bags filled with groceries in one hand and needed party supplies in the other.

"Geez, give me those bags," Chris laughed. "Did you remember to get ricotta?"

"Yes. I think we have everything. If not, it's too late. We don't have time to make another run to the store."

Darcy followed him into the kitchen. It was like the blind leading the blind, as neither had expert culinary skills. Opening a bottle of wine seemed like a great start. However, after a few glasses, Darcy was quickly getting inebriated.

"Why don't you decorate the living room. I've got this," Chris grinned.

After putting the finishing touches on the salad and garlic bread, he walked out to the living room. Gazing in horror, Darcy stood precariously on a ladder hanging a congratulations banner.

"Holy, hell, you're tipsy and on a ladder. Don't move," Chris laughed, running over to help.

Looking around the small room, it was a deranged display of party decorations. It was typical of Darcy to take her decorating skills to the unimaginable. Balloons, streamers, and banners had overtaken the entire space. Laughing hysterically, Chris knew Cassie and Chase would find it hilarious.

"Wow. You've been busy," Chris laughed, trying not to overreact at the sight of all the new décor.

"Doesn't it look amazing," Darcy giggled, reaching for more balloons.

"Well," he paused, trying not to offend his partner in crime. "I suppose amazing might describe it, but no more balloons, no more decorations. We have just enough time to put the ladder away and set the table."

Following Chris back to the kitchen, Darcy reached into the cabinets, searching for plates and cutlery.

"What? There are no matching plates or formal dinner wear."

"Darcey, you've eaten here before. It's only Chase and me, and you expect to find an elegant set of fine china. I'm sorry to disappoint you, Doll, but we're just a couple of broke lieutenants."

After setting the table and lighting candles, they had just a few minutes to admire their efforts before Chase arrived with Cassie. Finally, hearing keys unlocking the front door, they ran out to surprise the newly engaged couple.

"Surprise," Darcy yelled as the door opened.

"Congratulations," Chris added.

"Awe, the reason why you left work early?" Chase grinned, making his way through a sea of balloons and streamers.

"Thanks," Cassie smiled, hugging Darcy and then Chris. Then, focused on the overabundance of party décor, she snickered, knowing Darcy always took things to the extreme.

"Geez, Buddy, did you cook too?"

"Of course," Chris smiled.

After admiring Darcy's decorations, everyone made their way into the small dining room, where Chris served his delicious homemade lasagna. Afterward, Darcy brought out a cake she had purchased earlier at a local bakery. The evening was off to a great start despite the short time it took to prepare.

Lifting their glasses of wine, Chris and Darcy toasted their friends. Later, everyone retired to the living room.

"Thank you. It was a nice surprise," Cassie grinned, lounging back on the sofa in Chase's arms.

Later discussing their wedding plans and the fact Cassie's mother had persuaded her husband, the Earl, to come to terms with the idea, Cassie and Chase decided to call it a night.

"Guess we'll leave you two. Enjoy the rest of your evening," Chase smiled, grabbing Cassie's hand as he led her upstairs.

Getting into bed, he was thrilled to have Cassie all to himself. However, he noticed she appeared subdued and not her usual bubbly self.

"Sweetheart, what's wrong? You didn't appear exactly thrilled downstairs."

"Oh, Chase, trust me. I couldn't possibly be more excited about our engagement. It was nice of Chris and Darcy to go to such lengths to celebrate with us. I'm sorry. I don't mean to ruin the evening. It's the fact that my mom isn't doing well. Her kidney disease is getting worse, and it's becoming harder for her to undergo dialysis. In addition, she has an underlying heart condition that doesn't make her a candidate for a transplant. Chase, I don't know what I would do if something happened to her," Cassie explained, discreetly wiping tears from her eyes.

"Cassie, I'm sure your mother has the best doctors. I don't want you to worry. I'm always here for you. You know that, right?"

"Yes, but if something happens to her, I can't live with my father. I refuse to stay with that evil man. Mom and I have always been close, and she's excited about our engagement. She's my dad's complete opposite in every way. I don't understand why she married him. She'll never have what we have, a marriage based on love."

"Babe, I'm sorry. Please don't worry. You can always move in with me. That's an easy fix."

"Thanks, but I'll be there as long as Mom needs me. After that, I guess we'll wait and see."

Waking the following morning, Chase stared at Cassie. She appeared angelic as she slept peacefully beside him. She had finally fallen asleep after being awake most of the night with worries. Gently pulling her long curls away from her face, Chase lightly kissed her forehead. He knew that everything he ever wanted was lying next to him and that he would do anything to protect her from her father.

The following Monday, driving into the base, Chase and Chris felt exceptionally great after having an incredible weekend. However, they had no idea what awaited them.

Walking into the squadron, they expected a briefing on the day's schedule. Instead, an unexpected air of confusion filled the room. One glance at the perplexed state of those around them, and they knew something was wrong.

"Men, please have a seat," Colonel Graham solemnly remarked. "I know that most of you have been here for a few months. You've done one hell of a job, and I'm proud of your accomplishments since being here. Regrettably, due to the ongoing war efforts, many of you sitting here will be reassigned to Southeast Asia, specifically Vietnam. Also, most of you know that we lost Mad Dog last week. One hell of a guy, even though his personality preceded him. He'll be greatly missed. I have a stack of orders on my desk, which I will be passing out later today. Thank you again for your commitment to those who will be leaving. I'm sure your knowledge and skills will be a welcome addition to the Special Operations Squadron in Da Nang. Good luck."

"Oh my God," Chris silently mouthed, staring at Chase.

Later that evening, their worst fear was confirmed. The drive home was quiet. The fact that they had both just received orders to Vietnam was sobering.

"Buddy, I'm genuinely sorry. I know we both expected it, but the timing sucks for you. How will you ever break the news to Cassie?"

"Honestly, I have no idea. Cassie is worried about her mother. Her health appears to be deteriorating, and she has an underlying heart condition, which prevents her from receiving a kidney. You're right. The timing stinks."

Arriving at the tiny row house, they immediately walked into the kitchen. Grabbing two bottles of beer from the fridge, Chase tossed one to Chris. Lounging back on the sofa, he twisted the top from the bottle, taking a huge gulp.

"Damn, I think we're going to need something a lot stronger than beer," Chris suggested returning to the kitchen. Discovering a bottle of Jameson, he grabbed two glasses.

"That's more like it," Chase said, pouring himself a tall drink.

"How are you going to tell Cassie? What's your game plan? We only have a short time before we have to report for duty," Chris questioned, downing a huge swallow.

"I'm not sure. I might ask Darcy to let us stay at the beach house this weekend. It's private, and I'm worried Cassie will flip out."

"Well, Darcy and I could tag along. It might be a good idea. The girls are close, and hopefully, Darcy will keep Cassie from falling apart."

"I think you're right. Hopefully, Darcy could be the calm voice of reasoning. Unfortunately, it's a lot to put on her with her mother's current condition."

The following weekend the four of them arrived at the beach house. Neither of the girls was aware of the reason for the getaway. Bringing in bags of groceries, Chris had agreed to cook. Chase arranged logs in the fireplace, starting a roaring fire to warm the huge bungalow's bottom half.

"We need a bottle of wine," Darcy giggled, running into the kitchen behind Chris.

Cassie walked over, putting her arms around Chase. Then, looking down, she smiled, staring at the sparkling diamond on her left hand.

"Wow. I believe I made out like a bandit the last time we were here," Cassie reflected, lovingly caressing his face. "I love you."

"I love you too," Chase smiled with a wink.

Before the weekend was over, he knew the news he would give Cassie would utterly devastate her. Chase hated himself for hurting her.

Knowing that he had to tell her about the deployment for a millisecond, he entertained thoughts that maybe it would have been better that they had never met than hurt her. The timing couldn't possibly be worse, and the fact she had had a premonition made it even worse. Consumed with worries over her possible reaction, he knew this time would test their relationship, unlike the last time they were here. What if she decided she no longer wanted to be engaged? He couldn't blame her. However, he knew it would destroy him if she felt that way, and it definitely wouldn't be the right mindset for someone being deployed to war. He needed a drink. Something more potent than wine. It seemed Chris had read his mind as he walked out with a bottle of bourbon.

"Hey, Buddy, I think you could use a drink. I brought us something a little stronger," Chris remarked, handing Chase a glass of the amber liquid. "Here's to coming home safe. God be with us," he mouthed silently so the girls could not hear.

"Thanks." Chase downed his entire drink in one long continuous gulp, then taking the glass, he quickly poured another.

"Slow down, man. It would help if you were sober when you talked to Cassie. I don't think getting drunk before you break the news to her will be of any benefit. Save it for afterward in case things don't go your way. I put a pan of homemade lasagna in the oven, and I brought everything needed to make smores after dinner. I'll build a bonfire on the beach. Perhaps, a relaxing atmosphere will help. I'm here for you, Buddy."

Chilling thoughts of telling Cassie swirled through his mind. "Thanks, but I don't need your advice," Chase snapped.

"Just trying to help," Chris countered.

"Sorry, Buddy, it's all getting real, and telling Cassie has me tied up in knots."

Later that evening, after dinner, they gathered around a roaring bonfire on the beach, enjoying the simplistic taste of smores. Pulling Cassie into his arms, he lightly kissed her on the cheek. He knew he needed to break the news to her regarding his impending deployment. Staring into her eyes, she quickly sensed his fears.

"Babe, what's wrong? You've seemed edgy since we arrived."

Cassie had opened the door for the conversation. There was no turning back. Glancing at Chris, Chase knew the time had come. Taking a deep breath, he took Cassie's hand.

"Sweetheart, I love you. You know that, right?"

"Yes. I love you too. What's wrong?"

"I'm being deployed."

"What?" Cassie gasped in an absolute panic. Then, horrified, she quickly pulled away from Chase's grasp. "When?"

"In less than two weeks. I received reassignment to Da Nang Air Base in Vietnam. Chris and I both received orders." Waiting pensively for her response, he didn't have to wait long.

Instantly, fear utterly consumed Cassie. With tears streaming down her face, she stood up and began pacing. Staring at Darcy, I'm sure she expected her to confirm it was just a colossal misunderstanding. However, one glance at Darcy told her otherwise.

"Oh my God. I'm sorry," Darcy reacted, watching her best friend fall apart.

Before he could reach her and pull her into his arms, Cassie hysterically bolted down the beach.

"Chase, go after her," Darcy demanded.

"Damn, I don't need any more advice," Chase frowned.

Sprinting after Cassie, it appeared she had quickly gotten out of sight. Finally, Chase caught a glimpse of her in the darkness. Sitting on the beach, she had her knees drawn to her chest, appearing completely despondent. He slowly approached. Sitting next to her, he wrapped her in his arms, wiping tears from her face. Words seemed futile at a time like this.

"Sweetheart, I'm so sorry. I never meant to hurt you." Worried that he might lose her, Chase's eyes moistened.

"I know," Cassie bitterly sobbed. "I know, but I'm not strong. I don't know if I can do this," she cried, leaning into his embrace.

"Cassie, you're the bravest person I know, and we're going to survive the deployment," Chase replied, covering her with kisses. "I love you. I was so worried you might end our engagement when you found out."

"Chase, I love you. How could you even think I would do something like that?"

"Honestly, I couldn't blame you. However, if you did, so that you know, I would be totally destroyed. Cassie, I don't ever want to live without you."

"Chase, I want to build a life with you and raise a family. God willing, I want to grow old with you and one day tell our grandchildren how we met."

"Sweetheart, how did I ever deserve you. I love you."

"You better promise me one thing. It's all that I ask," Cassie sobbed.

"Anything."

"You better not die in that war. I can't lose you. My life doesn't work without you."

"Babe, trust me, nothing could keep me from you." Chase smiled, pulling Cassie up from the sand.

Wrapping his arms around her, they slowly made their way back to the beach house. Finally, the initial shock was over, and they were still engaged. Looking up at an abundance of twinkling stars, Chase whispered a prayer of thanks. Even though shell shocked, his girl remained steadfast in her commitment to their engagement.

Reaching the bonfire, Chris and Darcy had waited for their return.

"Is everything alright?" Darcy questioned.

"Yes," Cassie answered, not wanting to give further details. "I think Chase and I will turn in for the night. See you in the morning," Cassie added somberly. Then, grasping Chase's hand, she pulled him toward the house, leaving Chris and Darcy on the beach by the bonfire.

"Well, that appeared to go better than expected," Chris remarked.

"I'm not so sure," Darcy grimaced. "Why don't we go inside. I could use a drink."

"I have just what you need," Chris smirked.

"Oh, really, Lieutenant Sanchez, and what might that be?" Darcy giggled.

"Bourbon. However, I'll leave the rest up to you," he grinned wickedly.

Suddenly finding a soft spot in her heart for Chris, Darcy ruled nothing out. Thoughts of war and everything connected to it effortlessly, without thinking, enhanced her feelings toward him. So the fact they later went upstairs together wasn't a surprise. She knew friendships were a great precursor to romance. Sometimes, after receiving devastating news, another person's warmth kept the feeling of being alive worthwhile.

Reaching the bedroom and encasing themselves under the warm covers, Cassie snuggled next to Chase with her body tightly wrapped around him. "Are you scared?" Cassie worried.

"No, but, Sweetheart, I do have a few questions. First, what are your plans while I'm away?"

"Oh, you mean besides writing you tons of letters."

"Yes," Chase smiled, lifting long strands of curls away from the nape of her neck, kissing her softly. "I know the timing is horrible, and your mom is in declining health. But I'm worried about leaving you."

"I know. The timing stinks. If God forbid my mom doesn't make it through the next twelve months, I'm not staying with my father. I only stay there to take care of her," Cassie explained as tears welled in her eyes.

"Sweetheart, please don't cry. I hate what this is doing to you," Chase whispered, kissing away her tears. "What will you do if that were to happen?"

"I've already given this a lot of thought. I'm moving to New York to live with my Aunt Olivia. I've always dreamed of becoming a journalist. I'll stay with her until I can fully support myself or you're back in the states."

"Well, I'm somewhat surprised that you would leave England and Darcy. However, I totally support your decisions."

"Thanks. Glad to know that you're not going to be one of those controlling husbands."

"Babe, I wouldn't think of telling you what to do while I'm away. I'm excited to know that you will pursue your dreams. I've been fortunate to realize my dream of becoming a pilot, and I want the same for you. What are your thoughts regarding a family and babies? How many children do you want?" he smirked seductively.

"Lots."

"Well, maybe we should work on that."

"Slow down, Lieutenant Morgan, I'm on the pill, and there will be no talk of babies until we're married."

Turning off the light, Chase pulled Cassie into his arms. The night was young and off to a romantic start despite how it began. Craving every inch of her beautiful body, he gently caressed her face, kissing her passionately. Only a few short weeks remained before they would be on opposite sides of the world, and he didn't plan on wasting a single second.

As the morning sun peeped in under the curtains, Chase rolled over to kiss the love of his life. Sleep had once again eluded them. Instead, nights simply fueled their passion.

"Awe, good morning, Babe," Cassie smiled, rubbing her eyes.

"Good morning. Did you get any sleep?" Chase laughed.

"No, and I'm sure you're the reason."

"Geez, Sweetheart, I'll take that as a compliment," Chase grinned, giving her a quick kiss.

"Chris must be cooking breakfast. I'm starved. I smell bacon," Cassie exclaimed, bounding out of bed and grabbing her robe and slippers.

"Wow. I guess my plan of keeping you in bed all day isn't going to work," Chase frowned.

"Sorry, lieutenant, I need sustenance, and Chris is a great cook."

"If you insist," Chase scoffed, hurriedly pulling on a pair of sweat pants.

Walking into the kitchen, they stopped dead in their tracks, baffled by the scene unfolding before them. Wearing only a pair of black boxers, Chris stood at the stove frying bacon. Darcy was wearing one of Chris's shirts to add insult to injury, which completely swallowed her. She stood next to him, with her arms wrapped tightly around his waist.

"Oh my God. What's going on?" Cassie laughed hysterically.

"What? We're simply cooking breakfast. Hungry?" Darcy giggled.

"Oh," Cassie paused. "This is so not about cooking breakfast."

"Yeah, Buddy, what the hell is going on, and don't say cooking breakfast," Chase laughed.

"Well, if you must know, I guess it's fair to say that you and Cassie aren't the only ones who've hooked up since we've arrived."

"Geez, how long has this been going on?" Cassie snickered.

"Romantically speaking, just since last night," Darcy smiled. "However, I've had my eye on this guy for a long time."

"Isn't this sudden?" Chase questioned.

"Well, maybe," Chris grinned.

"Truthfully, knowing Chris will be deployed made me realize how much I care for him."

"You know, this is actually perfect. I'm happy for you and Darcy," Chase smiled. "Now, Cassie will have someone to commiserate with while we're in Vietnam."

"I'm happy as well. So you are together, right?" Cassie questioned, still confused by the incident.

"Yes," they both answered in unison, reading their minds.

"Well, I think this calls for a celebration," Cassie stated, reaching for a bottle of champagne and glasses. "Girlfriend, we need to talk."

"Later. Chris is cooking breakfast."

"How do you like your eggs?" Chris questioned with a smile.

"Cassie likes her's over easy, and surely you must know that I like mine scrambled."

The remaining weekend ended too soon as the four of them enjoyed the experience of being together as couples. Spending their last night around a bonfire making smores resulted in long hours of conversation. Finally, it was time to return to their daily lives.

Chapter Twelve

Cassie decided to move in with Chase until he left for Vietnam the following week. Even though it was against Earl Cromwell's wishes, he was confident their engagement would never materialize in a wedding. Knowing that Chase was on his way to Da Nang as an F-4 pilot, Cassie's father knew there was a good chance he might not return. However, he agreed to let Cassie move in with Chase without cutting her off from the family fortune, keeping his thoughts to himself.

Unfortunately, Cassie had no cooking experience, which resulted in many overcooked, burned meals the first week. Finally, Chris decided to cook each evening and save Cassie the humiliation. With Darcy's help, the girls, with some measure, managed to maintain the tiny house while the guys were at the base.

Chase and Chris were not required to be at the base the following week, giving them time to terminate their lease and vacate the premises. The beach house in Hunstanton seemed the perfect place to spend the remainder of their time.

Arriving late on a Friday evening, only two days remained. The guys were scheduled to fly out early Monday. Bringing in their luggage, Chase knew that Cassie was becoming emotional as he caught her discretely wiping her eyes. Pulling her aside, he held her in his arms.

"Sweetheart, you promised not to cry the entire weekend. We've just got here, and you're already becoming emotional."

"Chase, I'm only human. I'm sorry," Cassie wept. Burying her face against his chest, she knew this would be the most challenging two days of her life.

"Cassie, I love you, and it hurts to know that I'm the reason you're upset. But Babe, when I chose a military career, I knew there would be hardships. What I didn't realize was that it might affect someone else. I'm sorry."

"Oh, Chase, I'm proud of you and your career. I just need you to keep safe and come back to me. If I lost you, I'm not sure that I would have the willpower to go on with life."

"Hush, that's utter nonsense," Chase whispered, wiping her moist face. "Let's go inside and make the most of the time we have left."

"Okay. But don't ask me not to cry."

Overhearing their conversation and noticing Cassie's distress, Darcy walked over, hugging her.

"What am I chopped liver? I'm certainly not going anywhere, and I promise to be around to aggravate you each day until Chase is back safe and sound. That's my job as your best friend. Now, let's go inside and find something strong to drink."

"Thanks, Darcy. I love you."

"I love you too. Chase is right. No more crying."

"Who's hungry? I'm grilling some good ole American steaks tonight with all the trimmings, baked potatoes, baked beans, and salad," Chris announced.

"Great. I'm starved," Chase reacted, bringing in the last of the luggage.

Later that evening, after enjoying every morsel of the delicious meal and cleaning the kitchen, everyone decided to call it an early evening. It had been an emotional day.

"See you guys in the morning," Chris smiled, wrapping his arms around Darcy as they headed upstairs.

"Okay, Buddy, thanks for the meal. It was delicious."

Pulling Cassie down beside him on the sofa, he turned on the television. Searching through the channels for a movie, he hoped it would provide the perfect distraction for Cassie.

"What would you like to watch? I'll make popcorn."

"Oh, Chase, don't be silly. I'm not interested in watching a movie. Let's go upstairs."

"Wow, my kind of girl. I knew there was something I liked about you," Chase smiled wickedly, turning off the television.

Lifting Cassie from the sofa, Chase playfully put her over his shoulder, carrying her upstairs.

"Chase, you're crazy. Put me down," Cassie giggled.

"Yes, ma'am, as soon as I get you upstairs and into bed."

"Geez, Babe, I'm going to miss you," Cassie frowned.

"Well, just remember, it's not forever. I'll be back in twelve short months," Chase remarked.

Opening the bedroom door, Chase smiled. Placing Cassie on the bed, he dimmed the lights. He only had three nights to ravish her sexy body, leaving her without any doubts that his love would last forever. But, the memories made this weekend would have to carry them until he returned.

The following day Cassie and Chase once again woke to the aromas of breakfast coming from the downstairs kitchen. Then, hurriedly getting dressed, they bounded down the stairs.

"Geez, doesn't anyone ever sleep around here? Honestly, Chase, the animalistic sounds coming from your room last night could have awakened the dead," Chris grinned, pouring their coffee.

"Jealous?" Chase laughed.

"Awe, no," Darcy interjected. "Chris, must I remind you that you weren't exactly a monk last night."

"Okay, kids, enough talk about the nighttime activities in this house. Who wants blueberry pancakes?"

"That would be me," Cassie blushed, embarrassed by the crude banter. "Lots of butter and syrup."

Finishing breakfast, the next two days found them exploring the local community, taking long strolls on the beach, and enjoying the warmth of a bonfire each night under a plethora of stars. But, unfortunately, as the old saying goes, all good things come to an end. Monday morning arrived all too soon. Chase knew that he would have to remain stoic and unemotional for Cassie. Leaving her was going to be the hardest thing he had ever done.

Waking early to the sound of his alarm, Chase showered, shaved, and removed his military uniform from the closet, dressing in his blues.

Sitting up in bed, Cassie couldn't take her eyes off Chase as he quickly dressed. He had never looked sexier or more handsome. Watching as he splashed on a hint of cologne and buttoned the top of his blue dress shirt, she walked over, still wearing her sexy, black negligee.

Just the mere sight of Cassie as she walked toward him took his breath away. Pulling her close for a kiss, thoughts of leaving her destroyed him.

"Wow, Lieutenant Morgan, you look incredibly handsome this morning," Cassie smiled, trying to hold back a tsunami of tears welling within her eyes. "Chase, I have something for you. My grandmother gave me this silver cross before she passed. I've always worn it, and it has protected me over the years. Please take it with you."

"Sweetheart, are you sure you want to part with it?" Chase smiled, tenderly kissing her on the forehead. Taking the necklace seemed immature and childish. He wasn't sure he truly believed in such things. Still, if it meant something to Cassie, he would play along.

"Yes. I know it may seem silly, but I want you to have it."

"Thanks, Babe. If it means that much to you, I promise to keep it with me. Now, I think someone needs to get dressed if you and Darcy plan to drive us to the airport. We only have an hour before we leave," Chase winked, giving her another quick, passionate kiss. Noting the tears which were now softly slipping down her face, he bit his inner lip in an effort to remain stoic. Gently wiping the tears from her cheeks with the back of his hand, his heart was breaking. Whoever said grown men didn't cry was a fool. Chase knew he had to appear strong for Cassie, holding back a flood gate of emotions. If she witnessed him coming unglued, it would devastate her and make it almost impossible for him to leave. Chase was committed to a career, and their lives would forever be affected by his decision.

Arriving at the airport, Chase and Chris checked in their luggage. Then, they traveled together until they arrived in New York. Afterward, Chase was headed to Denver to visit his mom briefly, and Chris would be on his way to Miami. Then, finally, they would meet up at Da Nang Air Base in Vietnam.

Grasping Cassie's hand, she walked with him to the departure gate. With only a few minutes remaining before he boarded the plane, Chase prayed the next twelve months passed quickly. Thankful for Chris and Darcy's relationship, Chase was relieved that Darcy would be close, offering reassurance. Taking a seat in the boarding area, Chase held Cassie in his arms. Thoughts of leaving her were killing him.

Snuggled against Chase's muscular chest, Cassie knew he was determined to remain calm and composed. He would always be her confidant captain even through the most challenging situations, and today was the quintessence of challenging. Inhaling the fragrance of his cologne, visualizing his appearance, his smile, it would have to carry her until he returned. Only yesterday, Chase had walked into her life at the Boar's Head Pub, instantly changing her entire world. Now, fate was pulling them apart, and she was drowning in a sea of emotions.

"At this time, we will begin the boarding process for Flight 318 to Heathrow International. All first-class passengers and those needing assistance are welcome to board," the gate attendant announced.

Squeezing Chase's hand, Cassie froze. There were only minutes left before Chase would walk out of her life for a year. Losing control, Cassie was unable to contain her emotions. Burying her face against Chase's chest, she sobbed bitterly.

"Sweetheart, don't do this. You're my beautiful, strong girl. You've got this," Chase whispered, wrapping her in his arms.

"We are now continuing the boarding process for Flight 318. All passengers are welcome to board."

For the last time, Cassie hugged Chase. Then holding his hand in a vice-like grip, they walked toward the gate. As her fingers slowly slipped from his grasp, she felt like the air was being sucked from her lungs. Beneath her smile, she was dying on the inside.

"I love you, Flyboy."

"I love you too."

Watching as Chase slowly vanished from sight, this was by far the most challenging thing Cassie had ever done.

Walking over to the tall windows lining the boarding area, the girls watched as the plane carrying their loved ones slowly pushed back from the gate.

"How are you holding up?" Darcy questioned.

"Not good. I feel dizzy. I'm worried I might faint."

"Oh my God, sit down. Did you eat breakfast?"

"No. I was late getting dressed this morning."

"Well, that does it. I'm buying you lunch. Can you make it to the car?"

"I think so."

Once onboard the aircraft, Chris worried for his friend.

"Hey, Buddy, are you okay? I know that couldn't have been easy."

"Honestly, it was the hardest thing I've ever done. I could use a stiff drink. So what's the deal with you and Darcy? Is it serious?"

"Yes. I'm not sure if either of us saw it coming. Friendships can be an excellent place to start a relationship. At least that's what I've heard."

"Well, I'm happy for you. Darcy is a great girl."

"Thanks."

Discreetly reaching into his coat pocket, he felt the tiny silver cross.

Cassie and Darcy left the airport in silence and drove back to the beach house, stopping for lunch before arriving. Once back, Cassie ran upstairs. Removing her shoes, she slipped under the warm covers. Grabbing the pillow Chase slept with the previous night, she pulled it to her chest. It still held his scent. Snuggling with the pillow, Cassie could no longer keep her emotions in check. She cried a torrent of tears. Falling asleep from sheer exhaustion, she slept through dinner. Finally, fearing the worst, Darcy knocked on her door

"Cassie, are you okay?" she asked loudly. "I made bangers and mash. You have to try it."

"I'll be down in a few minutes," Cassie replied, feeling utterly crushed.

Later that evening, the girls built a bonfire in honor of the guys and roasted marshmallows. Without Chase and Chris, their lives had drastically changed. The following morning, Cassie moved home to care for her ailing mother, and Darcy returned home. After that, life became routine and simplistic.

The following weeks seemed to drag by after Chase deployed, then things took a drastic turn. Cassie's mom, Jaclyn, was hospitalized and given a grim prognosis of a few short weeks. Without Chase being there to offer love and support, Cassie was left with a tremendous burden. Her father remained completely insulate, unaffected by his wife's illness. It seemed more of a nuisance to him, and he appeared relieved that he might soon be rid of the daily confines of a terminally ill spouse. The only thing that kept Cassie going through this difficult time was her daily letters from Vietnam. They were her lifeline, the promise of their future together, and her only connection to Chase.

Cassie took on the added responsibility of planning a funeral upon her mother's passing. Her father's only assistance was monetary. Unfortunately, spending large amounts of money on the service, flowers, and elaborate headstone merely relieved his guilty conscious. As soon as her mother was laid to rest, Cassie planned to return to New York with her aunt. It would offer her a chance at a new life until Chase returned. Her letters to Chase were filled with the hopes of becoming a news journalist.

My Darling Chase,

Mom passed on Friday. It was peaceful, and I had to remind myself that she was no longer suffering. My Aunt Oliva came for the service, and I plan on returning with her. New York promises a new start in life until you return. I'm going to pursue my dream job, becoming a news journalist. Wish me luck. Babe, you have no idea how much I miss you. Living without you is truly the hardest thing I've ever done. How is Chris? Darcy misses him beyond words. I have to pack. We leave tomorrow

*morning. Please keep safe. I'll write as soon as I'm settled
in New York.*

*All my love,
Cassie*

Posting the letter in the mail felt cathartic. Finally, Cassie would no longer be under the confines of her father. She knew her father was finally happy to be rid of her and her mother in many ways. Cassie's only regret was leaving her best friend, Darcy. However, she promised to visit as often as possible.

Chapter Thirteen

Arriving in Vietnam, Chase and Chris were assigned to a Tactical Fighter Squadron. Life in Vietnam was fast-paced and kept them on their feet. They were always on guard for potential mortar attacks against the base.

Missing Cassie, Chase lived to receive her letters. Their correspondence was his lifeline to an outside world—a world that included their future. Having Chris along for the twelve months made life tolerable. Their connection to the girls kept life interesting, along with numerous nights of drinking.

"Hey, Buddy, my place later tonight. Cards and Jameson," Chris announced, tapping him on the shoulder as they walked into the daily briefing.

"Sounds good."

Flying F-4 Phantoms in Vietnam was hazardous. Unlike their routine training missions at RAF Mildenhall, the bombing raids over Hanoi, the Ho Chi Minh Trail, and other targeted hot spots were stressful. Their hope not to encounter North Vietnamese ground-to-air defenses or an airborne intercept was a constant worry. Delivering their payload and praying to make it back to the base afterward was always the goal. Their daily work routines were never mentioned in letters to the girls. They tried to shelter them from the fact that their deployment came with real dangers. However, it was impossible to know if the girls watched the war's ongoing news, which could be graphic. Off-duty hours in Da Nang came with lots of drinking, and tonight was no exception.

"Honey, I'm home," Chase laughed, walking into Chris's room in the barracks.

"Hey, did you stop by the Class Six Store?"

"No. You said you had Jameson."

"I do, but I was hoping you would pick up a couple of six-packs?"

"Geez, Chris, don't invite me over if you don't have the goods."

"Hell, it's a good thing I have an extra bottle," Chris mentioned, getting glasses and a deck of cards. "Ready to get creamed?"

"Buddy, that's not even a remote possibility," Chase scoffed, pouring himself a glass of Irish Whiskey.

"Did you get any mail from Cassie this week?"

"Yes. She's moving to New York."

"New York?" Chris choked, shuffling the cards.

"Her Aunt Oliva attended the funeral, and Cassie decided to return with her to the states."

"Wow. Really? Aren't you afraid she'll meet someone else and leave your sorry ass?"

"Geez, Buddy, thanks for the vote of confidence," Chase countered, downing a long slow swallow of the strong drink. "We're engaged, or has your demented brain forgotten?"

"Just saying. Cassie is a gorgeous girl with a royal title in front of her name. I'm sure New York is filled with guys who would love to be seen with her."

"Damn, Chris, keep your vindictive thoughts in that pea brain of yours, or I'm going to rearrange your face, and Darcy will never recognize you."

"Calm down, Buddy. Just throwing it out there," Chris smirked, pouring them each another glass of Jameson.

"I don't need your opinions. I trust Cassie," Chase vented, downing his entire glass in another long continuous gulp.

"Slow down. You're not passing out in my room."

Chris had made a valid point, and it was food for thought. It wasn't the fact that he didn't trust Cassie. It was the fact that he didn't trust other guys. However, being on the other side of the world for twelve long months caused him to worry. Cassie was beautiful, and he was sure she would easily catch the eye of anyone who saw her. Dismissing the ugly thoughts from his mind and focusing on the game at hand, it was utter nonsense.

Finally, Chase was ready to call it an evening, throwing down a winning hand at Pinochle. Then, grabbing the bottle of Jameson, he headed toward the door.

"Hey, that's my bottle," Chris yelled.

"Put it on my tab. Tomorrow is a down day. I'm going back to my room, kill the rest of this bottle, and hopefully pass out."

"Okay, Buddy, whatever helps you make it through the night."

Reaching his room, Chase lit a cigarette and poured himself a drink. Thoughts of Cassie with another guy were infuriating.

The next day, receiving another letter from Cassie completely lifted his spirits and filled him with confidence.

Hey Babe,

I miss you. It's so hard living without you. Even though I'm finally settled at my aunt's spacious three-bedroom apartment in Manhattan and applying for a New York Times position, it truly means nothing without you. I can't wait until you return and we start our life together. Aunt Olivia is anxious to meet you. She has offered to help us plan our wedding. I'm excited. She's taking me to try on wedding gowns next week. Even though our wedding is almost a year away, she said the planning would take months. No worries. I'll include you in all my decisions. I have to run. I promised to walk Augie and Baxter, Aunt Olivia's two Welsh corgis. Please keep safe. I've enclosed an envelope with my new address. I love you, Flyboy.

All my love,
Cassie

After reading and rereading the letter, how could he let Chris question their relationship? They were getting married as soon as his deployment ended. Reaching into his pocket, Chase pulled out the tiny cross pendant. One day soon, he would return it to Cassie, clasping it around his beautiful bride.

The following week they flew numerous bombing missions. It seemed that each day, a new target was issued. Then on Friday, the unthinkable happened. One of the F-4 Phantoms in their strike force took a direct hit. Luck was on their side as the crew managed to keep the plane airborne until they were out over the water, where they safely ejected. Later that afternoon, the post-flight debriefing made them aware of the dangers they faced daily. Heading directly to the Officer's Club, drinks flowed freely. Reaching his room, Chase felt compelled to write Cassie. Life was fragile.

Hey Sweetheart,

God, I miss you. I love you, and I can't wait until we're together again. The thought of seeing you in a bridal gown drives me crazy. Any ideas where you would like to go on our honeymoon? Trust me, after being away from your sexy body for twelve months, any place that has a bed will do. I'm relieved to learn that you are finally settled in New York with your aunt. She sounds like a wonderful woman, and I can't wait to meet her. I'm praying you received the internship. God knows you're the best applicant for the job. They would be lucky to have you. This will be short for now—a tough day. I'll see you in my dreams until we meet again.

Yours forever,
Love Chase

Life became a blur as one day turned into the next. Even amid the horrors of war, they settled into a daily routine. Things became repetitive: briefings, delivering a payload of bombs to specified targets, praying that they made it back to the base, post-briefings, and finally, the Stag Bar. Before they knew it, they had been deployed for six months. Then, the unthinkable happened.

Chapter Fourteen

Unbelievably, Cassie had been in New York for six months. She received the internship, which most days kept her busy. Cassie and her aunt were well into her wedding plans when the letters from Chase suddenly stopped. At first, she was sure it was just a glitch in the mail. However, after a month, Cassie was convinced something was wrong. She felt it. Then, Darcy came for a visit. Even though she was thrilled to see her, it was unexpected, and something seemed off about her sudden appearance.

"Cassie, dear, you have a visitor."

Running downstairs, she was excited yet apprehensive to see Darcy.

"Hey, Cassie, how are you? You look wonderful."

"Thanks. Come in. You remember my Aunt Olivia."

"Yes. How are you?"

"Fine, dear. Please make yourself at home. I'll leave you two. I'm sure that you have a lot of catching up."

"Thanks," Darcy smiled. "Cassie, can we go somewhere private to talk."

"Sure. There's a gorgeous park at the end of the street. We can stop for coffee. It's on the corner."

"Great."

Stopping for coffee, they continued to the park, where they found an empty bench.

"Darcy, what's wrong? I'm thrilled to see you, but it's unlike you to show up unannounced without telling me," Cassie questioned. "What brings you all the way to New York?"

"I don't know where to start or even how to tell you?"

"Tell me what? Please, you're making me nervous."

"Oh, Cassie, Chase's plane was shot down. He's listed as MIA, and it's doubtful that he survived. His plane went down under horrendous, hostile conditions in an area filled with Viet Cong Rebels. Chase and his weapons system officer were safely ejected. However, the wizzo was shot before his parachute touched the ground. Chase's chute opened, but unfortunately, he would have been surrounded by the Viet Cong.

"Oh my God, you're lying. Why are you saying this? I thought you were my best friend," Cassie replied in total disbelief.

"Cassie, I am your best friend. Why do you think I came here in person to tell you? I love you. I'm so sorry. Trust me, this is killing me."

"I don't believe a word you're saying."

"Cassie, think, when did you receive your last letter from Chase?"

"About a month ago."

"Cassie, Chase's plane went down about thirty days ago. They searched the entire area for his body or any sign that he might still be alive. Chris didn't want me to come until every last shred of hope that he might still be alive had vanished."

"Darcy, why are you doing this to me?" Cassie cried hysterically. "Why? Why are you deliberately trying to hurt me?"

"Oh, Cassie, I'm telling you the truth. This is by far the hardest thing I've ever had to do. I know how much you loved Chase. Chris is also having a hard time dealing with the loss of his best friend."

"I don't give a damn about Chris. Chase and I are getting married. I have my wedding gown."

With tears streaming down Cassie's face, she got up from the park bench and sprinted back toward her aunt's building. Concerned over her reaction to the dreadful news, Darcy chased after her.

Reaching the apartment, Cassie raced up to her room. Locking the door, she hurled herself on the bed. She cried rivers of tears. Losing her mom and now Chase, life held nothing for her. Chase was the love of her life, her safe place. She simply wanted to die. She had given him her grandmother's cross, and they were supposed to be married. Getting up from the bed, Cassie lost it. She began throwing everything she touched against the wall in a rage. She didn't want to be alive, and being destructive seemed her only release from the pain.

"My Lord, what's going on?" Cassie's aunt questioned, hearing the noise from upstairs, and stopping Darcy as she hurriedly raced into the apartment.

"Oh, I'm sorry for the intrusion. Unfortunately, Chase's plane went down," Darcy exclaimed. "I'm afraid he didn't make it, and I came to give Cassie the news. She's my best friend, and there was no way I would tell her over the phone."

"Oh, that poor child. We have to do something. She just lost her mother. This is too much," Olivia remarked, running upstairs to Cassie's room.

Cassie's aunt begged to be let in when she found the door locked. Finally, after a few minutes, Cassie unlocked the door. Entering the bedroom, Olivia walked over, simply holding Cassie in her arms as she sobbed bitterly.

"Cassie, Sweetheart, I'm so sorry. The news is truly unbelievable. Do you want me to call my doctor and have him prescribe a sedative?" she asked, looking around the room in shock.

"No. I just want to lie down."

"Are you sure?"

"Yes."

"I'll stay with her and make sure she's okay," Darcy suggested.

"Okay. I'll be downstairs if either of you needs anything."

"Thanks."

Taking Cassie's hand, Darcy led her over to the bed. Then, removing her shoes, she turned back the duvet and slipped her under the warm covers.

Watching Cassie drifting off to sleep, Darcy began cleaning up the room. Chris had been right about her coming to New York to give

Cassie the news. She couldn't imagine having told her over the phone and the trauma which might have ensued. Finally, taking a seat, Darcy couldn't take her eyes off her best friend. All the fun times they shared growing up, the evening at the Boar's Head when they met Chase and Chris, Monte Carlo, it all kept playing over and over in her mind like a movie reel. Finally, having found the man of her dreams, Cassie was young and in love. She didn't deserve this. Neither did Chase. What an unimaginable way to die. How was it possible for life to be so cruel?

After informing Cassie of Chase's untimely death, Darcy felt drained, becoming physically and mentally exhausted. Darcy felt drained along with the vast time difference. Deciding to curl up next to her best friend, she simply needed to shut her eyes and rest. Darcy had only been asleep for a short time when she was awakened by Cassie's moans and repeated whispers for Chase. Darcy's eyes welled with tears. Cassie was undoubtedly having a nightmare. Unfortunately, this nightmare held validity. Suddenly, Cassie bolted up from the bed.

"Oh my God, you're here. It's all true. Isn't it?" Cassie gasped.

"Yes. Cassie, I'm so sorry. I find it all truly unbelievable."

Holding her best friend in her arms, they cried incessant tears. There were no words of comfort. Words simply had no significance.

"Please don't leave me," Cassie pleaded.

"I will stay as long as you need me," Darcy offered, wiping her eyes.

The following week, Chase's mother, Carolyn, called. It appeared she had discovered Cassie's address and phone number in a letter that she had received earlier from Chase. Carolyn informed her that the family had no immediate plans for a memorial service. Even though they had never met, Carolyn was utterly sympathetic. It appeared that Chase had told his mother everything. The circumstance of their meeting, their engagement details, and how they planned to marry as soon as he returned. Cassie felt an immediate, unexplainable connection. Carolyn invited her for a visit. However, Cassie graciously declined. She needed time to heal and closure which would hopefully give her a new direction in life without Chase.

Over the next three years, Cassie worked hard to climb her way up the corporate ladder as a news journalist. No longer needing to rely on her family inheritance, she was self-reliant. Cassie reached the pinnacle of success at a relatively young age. Making a prominent name for herself in the world of journalism, the articles she had written drew wide acclaim. She traveled globally. Her photo with famous world leaders was often on the cover of prestigious magazines. However, despite all her accomplishments and accolades, one thing remained constant, her unwavering love for Chase.

Cassie's photo was often taken with men she dated and those accompanying her to corporate dinners and events. But, regardless of the fact, they meant nothing. Even though the sparkling diamond engagement ring was no longer an accessory, her feelings for Chase never changed. He simply owned her heart.

Chapter Fifteen

Chase slowly opened his eyes, waking with the worst headache of his life. Discovering he was restrained in leg irons on a concrete bunk, he gasped. His surroundings were horrendous. Roaches scurried across the dirty concrete floor of his cell. He was thankful to be alive. However, it quickly appeared that the bugs had a better life. They were free. A single light bulb hung from the ceiling, and the smell of human excrement hung heavily in the air. He was in a POW camp. However, it was impossible to know which prison or its exact location at first glance.

Wiping sweat from his brows, his recollections from the previous day ran through his mind like a horror movie. His F-4 Phantom had taken a direct hit from a surface-to-air missile. Instantly noting the degree of damage, Chase knew keeping his F-4 in the air long enough to make it safely to open water or the base wasn't in the realm of possibilities. The fact the plane was hit from the ground, he knew the chances of his survival and his wizzo making it out alive weren't exactly in their favor. Ejecting was their only hope of staying alive, and even that came with dire options. They were in hostile territory.

As Chase's parachute descended to the ground, he watched in absolute terror as his weapons system officer, Lieutenant Watkins, was shot on sight. Perhaps, being killed was a better fate than what waited for him on the ground. Thoughts of Cassie consumed him as he slowly drifted down to the jungle, which was crawling with Viet Cong rebels. Visions of seeing her in a bridal gown would most likely never happen.

Chase's nostrils filled with hot steam rising from the jungle floor and gun powder as he landed in a field of rice paddies. Instantly, he was surrounded by the screams of the rebels as they raced toward him. Undeniably, this was how he was going to meet his death. Reliving the scene made him cringe. The insurgents ran toward him with their AK-47s drawn and bayonets in hand. Miraculously, one of the soldiers decided to take him alive. However, his hands were bound, and he was beaten almost to the point of death before he passed out.

Chase's only thoughts were of Cassie as he lay on the hard concrete bed in the worst pain of his life. Perhaps dying in this decrepit hell hole was a better fate than Cassie being consumed with grief. Thoughts of her happily planning their wedding and now having to rebuild her life, which no longer included him, made him furious. How could a man know true happiness and discover that destiny had hurled him into utter despair? He no longer had Cassie's silver cross. It was lost forever in the rice paddies. But, perhaps, Cassie had been right. Maybe it was the reason his life was spared.

As the door to his cell opened, Chase's instincts told him it wasn't for his benefit. After his leg irons were unshackled, he was immediately hoisted from his bed and taken to an interrogation room, a nicer way of referring to a place of torture. Shoving him down on a stool, the soldiers asked for his rank, serial number, and the purpose of his mission. Refusing to comply, he was severely beaten and later subjected to the Vietnamese rope trick. Chase's elbows were tied together with rope behind his back, and he was restrained in leg irons. He remained in this position for hours and quickly lost the feeling in his hands. Chase had been briefed on what to expect if captured. However, nothing could have prepared him for the real atrocities of living in a POW Camp. Finally, they returned him to his cell, specifically his concrete bunk. Once again, he was restrained in leg irons, where he would remain isolated for days, weeks, and months.

Endless prayers and focusing on life outside the prison, life with

Cassie, his family, and even the thought of creature comforts kept him alive. Days and nights endlessly blended, keeping him in a constant state of fatigue and mental disorientation. Some days were better than others. However, each day was a complete struggle to survive.

Late one night, Chase heard the clear, distinct sound of tapping against his cell wall. Knowing he wasn't alone gave him some hope of surviving. Familiar with the tap code used inside the camp, he learned that he was housed inside the Hoa Lo Prison, aka the Hanoi Hilton. Learning to communicate with others through the systematic taps made life somewhat manageable if you could say that life inside a POW Camp was tolerable. Chase, along with the other prisoners, used this method of communication whenever possible.

Every night to keep his sanity, Chase mentally wrote letters to Cassie. Messages which she would never receive but which allowed him the intimacy of holding her in his dreams. They were his only connection to a girl he couldn't see, couldn't touch, couldn't hold close, but envisioned.

Sweetheart,

Thoughts of you are the only thing keeping me sane. Memories of our week in Monte Carlo and the Isle of Wight fill my lonely nights. I can see your beautiful smile, smell your fragrance, and feel the softness of your skin. The evening you came into the pub and walked into my life, I was the luckiest man on earth. I promised that I would come back to you. God willing, I hope to keep that promise. I have to believe that I will see you again and hold you in my arms. I have to think that I will meet you at the alter in your beautiful white gown, that we will raise a family, grow old together. Cassie, my love for you has no bounds. You're my first thought in the morning and my last each night.

Yours forever,
Chase

Chase could only speculate what coping methods the other prisoners used to stay lucid. At night he would lay awake, and after thinking of Cassie, his thoughts would turn to Chris. Hopefully, Chris made it back to the states. However, he had no way to know. He was in isolation, totally cut off from the outside world.

The meals which Chase ate were scarcely considered sustenance. They were simply to keep him alive. Cooked bitter greens and rice made up his diet. Often it might include unknown ingredients like rats, snakes, or insects. Over time he learned to appreciate even the most disgusting foods. In his mind's eye, he replaced every bite with Chris's homemade lasagna or Cassie's favorite, bangers and mash.

Chase was determined to make it out of the Hanoi Hilton alive. His faith, dreams of being reunited with Cassie, and the strength of those imprisoned made his survival possible.

Three years after entering the Hanoi Hilton, enduring the most formidable interrogations and torture, word came they were finally being released. At first, it seemed too much to hope for, but as each day passed, it became evident they were going home. Then in the spring of 1973, it happened.

Boarding a cargo plane, Chase was on his way to Clark Air Force Base in the Phillippines. This vital stop at a military hospital would provide weeks of recovery necessary to adjust. Acclimating to the real world and restoring his health was paramount. He had lost a tremendous amount of weight, and his body was riddled with sores. After his recovery, he continued to Denver to see his mother, Carolyn. He couldn't allow Cassie to see him in such a state. Resting at home was his only recourse before he tried to contact her. Having no idea what his future held, he only knew one thing, after seeing his mom, he would move heaven and earth to find Cassie. Hopefully, her feelings hadn't changed. However, unbeknown to him, his stop in Denver would provide the answers to most of his questions.

Chapter Sixteen

Arriving at the Denver International Airport, he touched American soil for the first time in three years. Catching sight of his mother, Carolyn, his breath hitched as he came through the jetway. He was home. Her smile contained three years of prayers, hopes, and dreams that her son was alive.

"Chase, Chase," Carolyn repeated as she ran toward her only child with open arms.

"Hey, Mom. It's so good to see you."

"Oh my God, Chase, let me look at you," she cried, pulling him into her arms. Caressing his face, she ran her fingers through his hair. "You've lost so much weight. Are you okay?"

"Yes, Mom, I'm fine," he smiled, embarrassed by her display of affection.

"Chase, I never gave up hope. Never. I knew you would come home. I prayed that God would keep you safe. I lit candles. I prayed the rosary more than I can remember," Carolyn wept.

"Mom, let's get you home," Chase grinned, wrapping her in his arms.

Driving out to the ranch, Carolyn talked nonstop. Unbelievably, she had her son at home, and there was so much catching up to do. Finally, everything was right in her world.

"Gracie, made your favorite meal, meatloaf with mac and cheese."

"Thanks, Mom," Chase laughed.

Gracie had been hired as a cook when he was much younger. Her name was synonymous with a good meal.

"That was sweet of her, but honestly, I'm exhausted, and there's a very comfortable bed upstairs calling my name."

"Well, you must eat first, then you can rest."

"Mom, have you possibly been in contact with Cassie during the past three years?"

"Yes. I've spoken with Cassie a few times, and I've kept up with her career."

"Career, what career?" Chase inquired.

"Chase, I suppose there was no way for you to know, but Cassie has made quite a name for herself in the world of journalism. She writes for one of the large newspapers in New York. I've saved many of her articles, some of which received worldwide acclaim. You can read them when we get home."

"Thanks. I'd like to see them before I turn in for the night."

"Okay. I knew you might. They're a snapshot of Cassie's life in journalism over the past few years."

"Do you know if she's still single or has a significant other in her life?"

"Sweetheart, I'm not sure. But, perhaps, the articles and photos will speak for themselves."

Oh my God, instantly, he fidgeted in his seat as anxiety overtook him. What was it that his mother wasn't telling him? What if Cassie had moved on with her life and found someone new. He had been considered dead for the past three years, and it would be perfectly normal for her to be married. What if she were married with children. She had wanted a large family. All the unknowns were enough to send him in the direction of a strong drink. Hell, he had been on a three-year dry spell. Tonight, he planned on reintroducing himself to a bottle of Jameson.

The sun was setting when they arrived at the Circle M Ranch. It was just as Chase remembered. His childhood memories came flooding back as they drove through the tall wrought iron gate with its enormous iconic insignia. Before his dad passed ten years ago, he had grown their herd of cattle to over twelve hundred. However, the ranch had been turned into a family venture maintained by his Uncle Sal since that time.

Their home had the appearance of a lodge rather than a personal residence as they entered the circular drive. Chase never understood why his mother chose to remain in a home of this size when she could have easily moved to a tropical island, avoiding all the harsh winters.

Grabbing what few bags he had, he walked into the foyer.

"Chase, I'll get those articles, but first, you must eat. Sweetheart, you've lost so much weight," Carolyn frowned.

"Mom, you worry too much. I'm going into the den to pour myself a drink. Would you like one?"

"No, thanks, it's too early for me. However, your Uncle Sal keeps the bar fully stocked.

Pouring himself a shot of Jameson, he tossed it back in one large gulp. Then, deciding to take the bottle upstairs to his room, he grabbed a glass from the bar.

"Chase, here are the magazine and newspaper clippings."

"Thanks, Mom. I'm sorry about dinner, but I feel incredibly exhausted. I'm going to turn in early. Thank Gracie for me."

"Sweetheart, you get some rest. I'm so thankful that you're home. But, honestly, I don't know what would have become of me if I had lost you," Carolyn cried.

"Mom, please, no more waterworks. I'm home, at least for the next few days. I love you. Maybe you should turn in early as well," Chase suggested, giving his mom a huge hug.

"I have a few phone calls to make. I promised to call your Uncle Sal when you got home. I'll see you in the morning. Get some rest."

"Goodnight. I love you."

Taking the bottle of Jameson and the articles regarding Cassie, Chase ran upstairs. Walking into his bedroom, he laughed. Nothing had changed since he graduated from high school and left for the Air Force Academy. His mother had practically made it a shrine in memory of her only son. Looking around, his trophies from baseball and track remained untouched. Pouring himself a tall drink of Jameson, he grabbed the magazines and clippings and sat on the bed. The softness of the mattress combined with the strong drink would be a force to reckon with as he tried to stay awake long enough to see what had kept Cassie busy the past three years.

Babe, what have you been up to? He smiled. Picking up the first magazine, he prayed he wouldn't discover another man's ring on her left hand. Turning to the earmarked page, he held his breath. Staring back at him, Cassie was surrounded by children in an African village. She looked radiant and happy. However, the photo gave him no view of her left hand. Tossing back another long continuous gulp of Jameson, he worried. Cassie's article was well written and depicted the urgent need for clean drinking water. He always knew she was talented. Great job, he thought, but damn it, he needed to see her left hand.

Anxiously picking up the next magazine, he quickly tore through the pages. Okay, Doll, what else have you been up to? Chase panicked, checking out the next set of photos. Unbelievably Cassie had covered the Munich Olympics Terrorist Attack in 1972, where an Arab gunman murdered eleven Israeli athletes. Babe, you weren't afraid to tackle even the scariest scenarios. That's my brave girl, he smiled, tossing back another shot. However, there was still no clear view of her left hand. Seriously, how was that even possible? Needing answers, he vented, pouring another glass of Irish whiskey. Turning the page, it highlighted Cassie being honored at an awards banquet for her efforts in covering the attack. However, there was no way to determine if her left hand was accessorized with a diamond.

Finally, picking up one of the newspaper clippings, he did a double-take as he stared at his beautiful girl. She was standing next to the mayor, and even though the photo was blemished and somewhat discolored, it appeared she wasn't sporting a ring on her left hand. That's my girl. Chase screamed loud enough to be heard by everyone in the house.

"Chase, are you okay?" his mom yelled up the stairs, worried he might be reliving some horrid torture he endured during his captivity.

"I'm fine, Mom, no worries," Chase responded.

Cassie had covered a story regarding the movement of the middle-class residents in New York to the suburbs. It had resulted in a loss of tax revenue for the city, which resulted in a severe fiscal crisis.

Folding the clipping, he put it on the nightstand. The following day, he was determined to fly to New York. There was no way he would stay in Denver after discovering Cassie might still be single and unattached. Even though his physique had definitely changed, he wouldn't let anything stand in his way.

Laying his head back on his pillow, Chase smiled. Only a four-hour flight stood between him and the love of his life. He had waited three long torturous years, and hopefully, he would be holding her in his arms in less than twenty-four hours. Considering the fact that Cassie probably no longer lived with her aunt, he decided to go straight to the newspaper where she worked. Sleep was elusive despite the luxurious comfort of sleeping in a bed and downing several shots of Jameson.

The following morning, as the sun's rays filtered in through the curtains, the smell of fried bacon and coffee sent him downstairs to the kitchen.

"Chase, your mom told me you were home. My God, son, it's so damn good to see you," Sal grinned, quickly putting down his coffee. Then, rushing over, he pulled Chase into his arms, giving him a huge hug.

"It's good to see you too. Trust me, I'm glad to be home," Chase smiled.

"How long will you be in Denver?"

"Not long, I'm afraid. In fact, I'll be leaving today."

"What?" Carolyn questioned, walking into the kitchen. "Chase, I was hoping you might stay for a few days. You promised?"

"Mom, I know, but I have to find Cassie. I'm sorry. I love you."

"Carolyn, our boy, has been away from that gorgeous girl for three long years. So don't make this difficult and stand in his way," Sal smiled with a wink.

"Thanks, Uncle Sal. You always were my favorite," Chase laughed.

Handing Chase a cup of coffee, Sal grinned. "I'll give you a ride out to the airport after breakfast. Are you packed?"

"Yep."

"Oh, Chase, are you sure?" Carolyn questioned, worried her son might get his heart broken.

"Mom, stop. I love you. No worries," Chase countered, giving her a quick kiss.

"Awe, my sweet boy," Gracie beamed, walking into the kitchen with a bag of groceries in tow. "Chase, thank God you're home," she grinned, walking over to hug him. "Your mother and I lit candles, and we prayed the rosary every day."

"I heard. Thanks. I suppose it worked," Chase smirked. Gracie was a strong Asian woman, and she had been a significant influence in his life since he was in grade school. He was glad that Gracie decided to stay on after his father passed. The fact that she didn't leave kept his mom from living alone all these years.

"You didn't eat my meatloaf and mac and cheese," she frowned.

"I'm sorry. I was rather exhausted when I arrived. Thanks for cooking. I'm sure as always it was delicious," Chase answered.

"I think we should let this young man eat breakfast before it gets cold. Then, I promised him a ride out to the airport," Sal smiled, knowing that if Chase stayed, he would be smothered by the women in the house.

Arriving at the airport, Chase bought the first available ticket to New York. Boarding his flight, he sat back in his seat. Thoughts of Cassie consumed him. By the day's end, he hoped to be holding the love of his life.

Chapter Seventeen

As the plane circled the city's outskirts on its approach to Kennedy International, Chase prayed that Cassie's feelings had not changed. Three years was a long time to wait for anyone, especially if there was no hope of him being alive. So he only asked God for one thing, a second chance with Cassie.

Hailing a cab into the city that never sleeps, Chase decided to make a reservation at the Plaza. He wanted to freshen up before he went to her office, and having a suite for the night might be the icing on the cake.

Checking in, he received his room key. Taking the elevator to the 6th floor, he unlocked the door. Living in a tiny cell for three years and sleeping on a concrete bunk, the Plaza suite offered sheer opulence. He only needed one person to make it complete. Jumping in the shower, he shaved and styled his hair. Finally, he spritzed on Cassie's favorite cologne and dressed casually in a pair of denim jeans and a T-shirt. Locking the door, Chase made his way to the elevator and out to the street to hail a taxi.

Arriving at the tall building which contained the New York Times where Cassie worked, he looked skyward, asking God for one last favor. Then, managing somehow to get past building security, he took the elevator up to the primary office. Stepping out of the elevator, he walked over to the receptionist.

"I'm here to see Cassie Cromwell."

"Sir, do you have an appointment? Is she expecting you?"

"No," he smiled.

"Well, I'm not supposed to allow visitors other than those with appointments."

"Trust me. I think she might make an exception."

"Against my better judgment, you can go in. If Miss Cromwell is not in her office, you might find her in the breakroom at the end of the hall."

Walking down the expansive narrow hallway, he didn't have far to go before finding her office. Taking a second to compose himself, he held his breath. This was it. There was no turning back. After three long years, they were about to be reunited. Slowly, opening the door, he entered her office. There was no sign of Cassie. Evidently, she was in the break room, as the receptionist suggested. Running down the hall, he once again held his breath as he walked in. Quickly surveying the entire room, she wasn't there. There was no one that even remotely resembled Cassie.

"You look lost. Are you looking for someone?" a young woman asked.

"Yes. Cassie Cromwell."

"Well, you just missed her. She walked down to her favorite coffee shop at the end of the street, Manhattan Mocha. You can't miss it."

Racing to the elevator, Chase made his way down to the lobby. A brisk wind disheveled his hair as he stepped outside. Then sprinting toward the end of the busy street, his heart was in his throat. He couldn't wait to see her. Seeing a sign in the distance for Manhattan Mocha, Chase hurried faster, picking up his pace. If there was a chance she was there, he didn't want to miss her. Finally, stopping outside the coffee shop, he glanced through the large glass window. Cassie was standing at the counter. His heart raced as if it would explode at the mere sight of her. Pausing for a second, he ran his fingers through his hair. She was alone and more beautiful than he had ever remembered. Holding his breath, he walked in.

"May I buy you a coffee?" he smiled.

With trembling legs, Cassie recognized his voice. Turning around, she came face to face with a ghost. Dropping her coffee, she felt faint. Slowly, in disbelief, she smiled, "Of course, lieutenant, what took you so long?" Cassie cried, reaching up to touch his face.

"Sweetheart, you're hard to find."

"Oh my God, Chase," Cassie sobbed, jumping into his arms. Then, oblivious to the patrons standing in line, or the spilled coffee, Cassie wrapped her arms around Chase. "I thought you were dead?"

"Babe, do I look dead?" Chase teased.

"You've lost so much weight."

"Minor details."

Holding up the coffee line, Chase held her in his arms, kissing her with an extreme passion too intense for a viewing audience. As their kiss lingered for minutes, the young lady waiting next in line to order smiled.

"I'll have some of that," she giggled, approaching the barista.

Finally, breaking from their kiss, Chase whispered. "I have a suite at the Plaza. Let's go."

Scooping Cassie into his arms, coffee was a forgotten detail. Chase motioned for a cab, carrying her outside to the busy street corner.

Helping Cassie inside the car, Chase pulled her into his arms.

"God, I've missed you."

"I missed you too," Cassie wept, leaning her head against his chest.

As the cab pulled away from the curb, Cassie lovingly caressed his face.

"What possibly kept you alive?" she whispered.

"Thoughts of You."

Epilogue

"A December wedding will be perfect," Olivia announced. Her zest at helping plan Cassie's wedding was finally a reality. She had waited three long years to see her niece marry the man of her dreams. "I guess we're just missing the maid of honor and best man," she added.

Looking at Chase, Cassie smiled. "Oh, I think we have two people for those positions."

"Yes," Chase agreed. "We just have to fly them over to the states."

Chris and Darcy married when Chris returned from his deployment. Darcy knew that life was short. They welcomed their first child, Christian Michael Sanchez, nine months later. Overjoyed to be included in the wedding party, they couldn't wait to be reunited with their friends. At Darcy's insistence, Chris decided not to reenlist. Now living in Cambridge, they couldn't be happier.

"One last thing," Chase mentioned.

"Oh, I thought we had everything covered," Cassie questioned.

"Where would you like to go on our honeymoon? Just name it. Any place in the world will do as long as there's a bed," Chase winked wickedly.

"Chase, there's only one place that comes to mind."

"Really? That was quick."

"The beach house in Hunstanton."

Needless to say, the wedding went off without a hitch.

Life was finally good as they sat together on the beach near a roaring bonfire under a brilliant canopy of shimmering stars.

"So, Mrs. Morgan, refresh my memory. How many children do you want?" Chase smirked.

"Lots."

Grasping Cassie's hand, Chase pulled her toward the beach house. Being an only child, he couldn't wait to fill their home with the boisterous laughter of children.

Deciding to make the military a lifelong commitment, Chase retired with the rank of Lieutenant Colonel. Cassie continued her journalism career by writing for local newspapers. Raising their large family, two sons, who graduated from the Air Force Academy, and three gorgeous daughters, who exemplified their mother's beauty, life was an adventure.

After traveling worldwide for over twenty years, they finally settled in Cambridge near Chris and Darcy. Unbelievably, the Earl of Cromwell discovered a new title. After years of living alone without family, he preferred the joys of simply being called grandpa.

Looking down, Jaclyn smiled. At last, Cassie was happy.